A Monotonous Landscape

A Monotonous Landscape

Seven Stories | Günter Herburger

Translated by Geoffrey Skelton

A Helen and Kurt Wolff Book

Harcourt, Brace & World, Inc., New York

Contents

Monte Prisu

There wasn't a single room left in Damüls, nor in Brigg, let alone in Sollern, so he drove straight to Ranzonso at the other end of the valley, passing Schwengen, Kammers, and Au on the way. Ranzonso is border country, and its other name is Ranzern. Behind it there is not even a pass, only the ski lift that goes up the Beluga. At the top, just beneath the upper station in the middle of the steep slope, was the starting point for the spring races.

Dolterer tried again at the travel bureau there, but the people only laughed. He should have applied in the autumn: everything had been booked up for weeks. So he slept in the car, the seat turned back so that he could stretch out his legs. Each time he woke up, stiff with cold, he thought of the final exams, which he had just passed.

The following morning he walked around behind the church, not wanting to be seen by any of the skiers, who always put up in the Casino. Harlacher's boardinghouse was reserved for the ladies. Harlacher was President of the Ski Club.

Dolterer deposited his skis, poles, and boots in the cellar of the station buffet which the council had built near the bottom of the ski lift. Then he went inside and sat down at the best table, which looked out over the final downhill run and the forest track above, which was called the Cannonbarrel because it was as straight as a gunbarrel and had the same velocity. And he found himself thinking again about his exam.

He had started off with short poles and special black epaulettes decorated with a metal edelweiss. That had been the fashion then. The shorter the poles, the more dashing the skier. Dolterer was the only one from his town on the instruction course. Their rucksacks stuffed full of potatoes, they had boarded the train: the big shots from the SS cadet college at Sonthofen in the first carriage and the rest farther behind in small groups, those who spoke the same dialect always together. The Napola Cubs wore black tapered slacks and black shirts, but they had rotten ski bindings. Dolterer had some special Norwegian wax with him—a present from his grandfather; you had to burn it into the running surface of the skis over a wood fire. His bindings were first-class, a combination of leather and metal spring fastenings. Only the proper ski aces had anything like it. He could lean forward on straight legs, ever so slowly, until his nose was touching the tips of his skis, and then straighten up again. All the others were deeply envious.

They arrived in Ranzern in the dark, when the lift had stopped running. They were met by a man who looked like a lumberjack. He said, "Heil'tler!" and immediately after that "*Sakrament*," much to the annoyance of the Sonthofen crew, who as the train was coming into the station had flung down all the windows and stretched their arms out stiff as pokers in the Hitler salute.

In spite of his baggy breeches, this man said he was their ski instructor and chased them through the night up to Harlacher's house. Their skis on their shoulders, poles crossed underneath to keep the bindings from digging in, they climbed uphill for a full hour. The potato-filled rucksacks pulled at their backs and it was cold, but they sweated, hung out their tongues, and swallowed their thick saliva. There were hard-crusted humps of snow and washboards everywhere, and their boots broke through or skidded on icy track marks. None of them knew where they were going, but they followed each other up the mountain, a panting, snaking column. Dolterer was somewhere in the middle, which made things a bit easier.

The instructor August Feranello—he had barked out his name to the Sonthofen boys at the station—was at them at both ends of the column. He burrowed through their ranks, shouting at those who staggered off the track, taking over skis and rucksacks, gathering the weak to him and howling out his "Heil'tler!" as he pushed through the Napola Cubs. It was two in the morning by the time they reached the Harlacher house. They were given hot tea before they flopped down on the straw mattresses. Dolterer's head was resting on somebody's stomach, but he was too tired to lift it. He fell asleep in the middle of drawing a breath.

Next morning Feranello and a second instructor called Raspe, who spoke with an educated accent, made them ski down the steep slope behind the house one after another through ten slalom gates. Every time somebody hit a pole Feranello cried out, "Oh, the Heil'tler!" and "Come here, you." Then he took his group off to the beginners' slope beside the bottom station of the lift, while the more advanced ones went with Raspe up the Beluga. During the whole course the use of the ski lift was free.

"You must keep at it and watch your forward positions," Raspe told them. "But first we must get you familiar with the slope."

He took them over it twice in sections, pointing out the route and showing them how to negotiate the moguls. That was the whole extent of his instruction. From then on he just called the roll in the morning before sending them out on the trail. Dolterer was very disappointed: he had not expected the alpine training center to be so tame. Back home there had been one test after another covering a full six months—gymnastics, map-reading, history, strategy—and he had had to write two papers. All that on top of school and training. But here nobody seemed to take anything seriously.

The boy on whose stomach he had lain that first night was called Kurt Zwiesel. When he skied everything shook. He knocked over slalom poles, catapulted through the other skiers, but always kept on his feet. He had no technique, but plenty of power.

Dolterer found him irritating, for it sometimes happened that on the downhill run Kurt put in the better time. Technique did not help him then, no amount of forward leaning or tailwagging, crouching or hopping daintily over moguls. Dolterer was thrown, while Kurt, suspended shockingly in the air, wobbling from mogul to mogul, crashed down, tore a wide track across the trail, but stayed on his feet.

"Step on it, you oaf!" he would cry from the bottom, standing there red-faced and panting, while Dolterer carefully traced a tidy turn across the last rise. "Hurry up, get your ass in gear."

"You'll never get anywhere," Dolterer said, brushing shreds of snow from his trousers. "You've got no style."

"What haven't I got?"

He was not to be shaken off. On the lift he hooked onto the bar right behind Dolterer and, as they were hauled up, yodeled and guffawed until all the people doing cautious kick turns on the trail stopped to look at them.

After four days Dolterer knew every inch of the downhill run. He knew where to start a turn and where to let himself be carried out of the turn around the next curve. Instructor Raspe was never there. Before the morning period ended he was off to the village in his highland uniform, a white silk muffler tucked beneath the open collar of his jacket. Dolterer once saw the cook give him a little carton of honey substitute. Down on the beginners' slope Feranello was chasing the Sonthofeners around. He stood halfway down the slope, made them ski past him in turn, shouted out commands and snarled at them if they did not at once start climbing back up the hill. Their uniforms were soaked through and rumpled, and they made no murmur when Feranello called them a bunch of yellowbellies. Three times during the week they had political instruction in the common room. Each time Raspe told the Sonthofen group leader to read aloud a chapter from *Mein Kampf*, and then he went off. Zwiesel at once got to his feet and said loudly, "He's gone to stuff his girl again." Dolterer wanted to hear what the group leader was reading, but everyone was bawling, and then the group leader himself was up on a chair, letting his green lanyard hang from his trouser flap and wagging it back and forth.

Next day Dolterer said to Zwiesel, "I'm going up Monte Prisu. I'll go alone if you don't want to come." Monte Prisu was the mountain directly adjoining the Beluga saddle, a long steep flank of dwarf pines and rocks and after that nothing. On the other side of the mountain, topped by fluttering pennants of snow, there was probably Italy.

Zwiesel went with him. Nobody would notice if they went off for a day by themselves. They took bread and canned meat with them, as much as they could stuff into their pockets.

There were people sitting in deck chairs at the Beluga top station, their faces smeared with grease, which soon gave them blistered complexions the color of boiled crabs. Above the lift they fixed skins to their skis and began to climb. Dolterer went first. Now he could really show what he could do, the delicate fourteen-year-old lad with his sloping swan's shoulders, his billiard-ball head under the motorcyclist's cap, flaps sticking out like bat's ears and jogging up and down in rhythm with each step. He climbed at a steady pace, tracing one hairpin turn after another across the slope, never too steep and never too shallow, the angle exactly as it should be, covering the whole length of the slope right out to the drifts which fell off into the east and west valleys. At that point he would make a textbook turn, reversing the upper ski and putting it down on the track behind, then, supporting himself on the downhill pole, bringing around the other ski in a backward turn. The more he sweated the stronger he felt. He blew the drops off the end of his nose, his poles moving in regular rhythm. Behind him came Zwiesel, cocksure as ever, and wanting of course to talk. He started in again about Raspe's girl friend, puffing and dribbling and having to stop to regain his breath. But now Dolterer no longer cared. He moved steadily on, not even turning his head.

"I know who he's laying," Zwiesel called out suddenly, from the turn below, while Dolterer laid a track over a stretch of old snow. "It's Harlacher's daughter. Her husband was blown sky-high in the Caucasus. And her father doesn't mind, because he's got another daughter and because we're staying in his house. He's getting the rent—and besides, he's scared, because he's a smuggler. Feranello's in it too. They're off over the Beluga every night."

Dolterer was now three turns above him. Zwiesel suddenly broke into a gallop, clambering straight up through the tracks until he was once again close behind.

After two hours Zwiesel was no longer talking, and he stayed in Dolterer's tracks. They had left the dwarf pines behind and were climbing on ledges of snow between the boulders. The ledges were at times so narrow that they could only mount in diagonal steps. Then, beyond the rocks, they could get no farther. From below they had not been able to see how steep the slope really was. All they could do now was take off their skis and climb up across the slippery snowfield. They sat down on the edge of a gully and stared upwards.

"Come on, let's go," Zwiesel said.

"Shut up," Dolterer hissed. "You'll start an avalanche."

"Where? I can't see anything."

"There're cracks in the slope," Dolterer breathed. "The snow slides off the ledges. Another step and we'll be dumped into the valley."

"How do you know?"

"Everybody knows that."

"Where are the cracks?" Zwiesel whispered.

"Don't move."

Zwiesel sat stiff and upright, his head a bit to one side so that he too would see when the avalanches came. Dolterer blinked up into the sky, sure that he was right. There was no such thing as a Monte Prisu without avalanches.

Below them, on the other side of the vast snowfield over which they had climbed, they could see the bottom station of the ski lift with a lot of little dots scattered around it and, still lower down, where the valley made a round curve, the first houses of Ranzern, hardly visible in the haze. And here they sat miles above, threatened by avalanches, staring at the peak to which no lift went and beside it other peaks where there was nobody—peaks which only they could see and count and

put names to, such as Piz Mormasch, Rattenkopf, and Gra-
natenberg, and which were all much more dangerous than they
looked beneath the snow.

"I have to take a leak and I'm hungry," said Zwiesel.

Dolterer took some bread and a can of meat from inside his
jacket and silently handed them over. Zwiesel started to break
the can open with the point of his ski pole.

"Not so loud, you fool!"

"Nothing'll happen," Zwiesel said, and suddenly shouted
"Hey!" and "Get a move on, snow!" Singing, he seized the can
and kept banging it against a rock.

And as the wall of snow above them stayed peacefully where
it was, Dolterer himself began to bore at a can until he had
made a hole big enough to poke his fingers in and scratch out
the fatty pork. He bit off some bread, chewed it carefully, then
helped it down with a pinch of meat. And all the time he kept
his ears open for the tiny dry ping of an impending avalanche.
Zwiesel had cut his finger on the edge of the tin. He was letting the blood drip on his bread, and then he ate it.

"Shall we take off, Kurt?" Dolterer said.

"Wait a bit, let's see who can hit farthest."

They positioned themselves on a jutting rock, but the wind
bent the thin jets to the left, and Zwiesel hit Dolterer on the
trouser leg.

"It's no good here," he said. "We'd better go behind the
rock."

There it was sheltered from the wind, and the snow was
smooth.

"I can do a figure six," Zwiesel said. He began at the top,
traced a frayed yellow downward curve and then drew it
around to form a shaky bulbous O, which got fuller and fuller
around the middle and turned into a dish full of holes, for
Zwiesel had too much inside him—enough for a one or any
other number.

Watching him, Dolterer lost control, did not wait for Zwiesel
to finish, and started, but with too much pressure, so that he
botched the beginning of his V. Above and below it he drew

two thick bars, then cut off resolutely and traced three vertical lines side by side, the last only just completed with a final spurt.

"What's that?" Zwiesel asked.

"It's a Roman eight," said Dolterer.

"Honest? I've never heard of those," Zwiesel said. "So we're buddies now."

Then they shoved off.

In half an hour they were back down in the valley. Nobody had ears for them. Everybody was jostling about a large jam jar standing on the table, and Feranello told them to get cups for some punch. In the kitchen they found Raspe, who told them that the war was over.

Seated at the window of the lift station buffet, Dolterer finished his second glass of tomato juice. He became fidgety when he saw some people come out on the Cannonbarrel. They were placing the slalom posts on the final run. Others were stretching dividing ropes to each side of it, placing tables at the bottom for the judges, and looping cable for the amplifiers over tree branches with long forked poles. The lift had begun to move, too. People were being hauled up, armed with spades. They would be banking up the dangerous curves on the run. Some skiers whom Dolterer knew from earlier occasions appeared around the corner of the house. He turned away from the window and tried to make himself small.

They were Sepp Maschlings, a cabinetmaker from Innsbruck, and Ludwig Kalb from Frankfurt, whose father owned a cotton factory. Jean Rapponard was there too—still around on the ski trails, though he was well past thirty. Seven years ago he had invented a new skiing style, which nobody used nowadays except Rapponard himself. However, it still brought him regularly in to somewhere about tenth place.

The three of them sat down at another table near the big picture window and ordered tea. Since it would hardly be possible to slip past them without being recognized, Dolterer plucked up his courage, got to his feet, and went over to the other table. "What time does it start?" he said, smiling.

"Look who's here! Babe Dolterer!" they all exclaimed in unison. "What are you doing here? Are you in the race?" They edged up and made room for him to sit beside them.

"No, I'm not competing," Dolterer said. "I've passed my final exams, and wanted to see the spring races once again before starting my job." He started to tell them how hard he had worked since he entered the races for the last time four winters ago. The whole family had put money into him. His aunt had sent him a weekly food parcel from her grocery shop in Regensburg, his father had got himself transferred from the town hall in Kaufbeuren to a job in the State Archives in Munich so that he would not have to pay rent for a room, and his mother had taken in lodgers in the new apartment. "My studies left no time for training," he concluded.

"But you'll come along with us today?" Rapponard said.

"I'm not entered, and besides I'm not in form."

"That doesn't matter," said Rapponard. "We'll all go slower. Then it won't show."

"Yes, we'll do that," Maschlings said.

And Ludwig Kalb added that the Ranzonso race was of no great importance to them now. They had none of them done very well in the European championships this year. There were some very young skiers about who were fast, if lacking in method. He was getting tired of the whole business: it was always the same old grind.

There was a pause. They were all busy with their thoughts. Ludwig Kalb started off again. Two years ago he had spent an August training on Monte Rosa, and afterwards his father had taken him to Chile, where he had given some demonstrations. They knew nothing about modern slalom methods out there.

"But you haven't had a first in slalom since the Kannenwind races three years ago," Dolterer said.

No, since then Maschlings had taken over, but he was still good for a few second or third places.

Maschlings was married now. He was leaving Innsbruck, since his wife's father had a furniture factory somewhere in Württemberg. He was going to try to talk his father-in-law into manufacturing skis; then each win he made would bring in business. "But I'm not making a thing of it," he went on. "My wife's expecting a baby. I'll do some skiing whenever there's a chance, but I'm not all that keen any more."

That was Maschlings all over. Nothing mattered much to him. If he fell he would give up at once and cruise, whistling, down to the finishing line, where the competition organizer would snarl at him, for no one gives up till bones are broken. Yet maybe only a week later he would come through with a first.

"Look here, Babe Dolterer," Jean Rapponard said, "we're just going along to see Harlacher. We'll tell him you're coming with us."

"It's much too late to enter now."

"You know Harlacher and I know Harlacher. He'll do it if he feels like it."

"I'm not coming," Dolterer said.

"Harlacher knows I spent a couple of winters as a ski instructor in Flüelen," Rapponard continued, "as well as on a professional tour in America. But he's letting me start all the same. Harlacher needs names for his race, and it doesn't count in the championships, as you know. Maybe the Austrians are sometimes a bit better than we are, but who has ever heard of them? You had a name—second in Europe and once a member of the Olympic team. Harlacher can announce all that over his microphone, and so he'll let you in. Come along, let's talk with him."

"I'm not coming," Dolterer repeated, staying firm in his seat. Rapponard and Kalb exchanged glances and stood up. They told Maschlings to keep an eye on him until they came back.

"When does the race start?" Dolterer asked after they had gone.

"At two," Maschlings said. "There's plenty of time. I've already been here a week. The course is in excellent condition. I'm almost overtrained, with one race after another. You'll be able to keep up, you'll see."

Maschlings was trying to get him into the right mood, and Dolterer hadn't the will power simply to get up and go. It's all very well, with your finals in the bag, to say count me out, but such a long-standing ski comradeship as theirs does mean something, after all.

"I've lost the touch," he said.

"It's something you can't lose. Once you're at the starting gate your body takes over. You'll be off down the slope the way you used to."

"I've got no skis," Dolterer said.

"I've got four pairs, and Rapponard always carries a pile of boots around with him. What's the matter? Scared?"

"I suppose so," Dolterer said.

"Who isn't?" Maschlings replied.

They stayed there waiting. Out on the slope there was a lot going on: people everywhere and the lift in full use. The waitress in the buffet was getting all the orders mixed up. Everyone was talking about the race, the snow conditions, the favorites, and the hazards of the course. They went on drinking tea.

In the years before his graduation Dolterer had been eager in his training. Whenever he could get away from school he had taken part in every race. Once he had almost failed to graduate, but in the spring, when the strenuous skiing season was over, he had managed to catch up again. In the summer he did a lot of swimming and running in the woods and skipping every night. You had to keep in condition all year round if you wanted to stay in the game.

Four months before his graduation he had been in Ranzonso again. It had got to be a custom for all the top set to meet there at the end of winter for a final fling. That year the Americans were there too, as well as a Japanese slalom expert.

The village which had formerly been called Ranzern had now become famous. New hotels had sprung up in the valley, and the road across the flat stretch from Damüls had been asphalted. There were always a lot of visitors, for the wide mountain valley got plenty of sun, and the weather barrier of the Dolomites lay farther to the north. A new fast lift had been built up the Beluga. Where the old lift had been was now the downhill course following the fall line from top to bottom station. It provided a murderous run, and Dolterer was too light.

"You could pour a disk of lead into your skis," Zwiesel had told him, "just under the bindings. I've seen Rapponard doing speed trials on the Toblach glacier with a wind sleeve on his back to stabilize him. It looked like a speedboat coming down. He had jumping skis with three grooves, all filled up with lead. That held him down on the ice."

Zwiesel of all people to give him advice—Zwiesel, who skied like a lumberjack!

"That would unsettle the ratio between my weight and the weight of my skis. I'd only be able to ski in a straight line."

"That sort of ratio doesn't mean a thing," Zwiesel said.

"Strength alone is not enough," Dolterer said. "You must think with your knees and ankles too."

Zwiesel laughed till he choked. "Nuts," he said. "Either you make it or you take a spill."

"You don't have to take a spill. But that's something you'll never understand. It's a miracle they let you loose at all."

"Yes, it is," Zwiesel replied, and now he was not laughing. "Sometimes I just shut my eyes because it's all so fast."

They were both staying in the annex to Harlacher's house. The Ranzonso Ski Club was paying their expenses. Dolterer had been all over the place in the last few years, had got to know a lot of people, and curiously enough was always meeting up with Zwiesel, who managed to keep in the top class, though always one of the also-rans. The more difficult the race, the more unpredictable was Zwiesel's performance. He worked during the summer at the freight yard in Dornbirn, where his father was a shunter. Watch it, Zwiesel's coming, the other skiers would tell each other, knowing that the oddball from somewhere in Vorarlberg with his duck's nose and spiky hair always pointed his skis straight at the shortest route and shot off down it regardless. As a rule he ended up in the trees or mowed down the slalom poles one after another, but if he did make it it could happen that he turned in the fastest time.

Ever since their trip up Monte Prisu Dolterer had wanted to

teach Zwiesel style, or at any rate to make him know what fear was, for otherwise he would never get anywhere, even in his own peculiar way. But Zwiesel would not catch on. He mixed up parallel with jump turns, wore skis too short for his height and sometimes lost hold of his poles, on which the leather loops were mended with thin string. Not only that, but he also tried out other techniques, just for the fun of it, which is bad for the body habits.

One winter he gave up the slalom entirely and made up his mind to master the Scandinavian combination. The idea struck him all of a sudden when he was busy shunting freight cars in Dornbirn. With no training at all he had entered for the first cross-country run of the season, a fifteen-kilometer race across flat country. He knew nothing of either the Finnish or the Norwegian technique. He simply pushed through, bellowing as he overtook or even forcing the man in front off the track, which is considered a mortal sin. When he got winded he just stopped until he had his breath back again. Once during a race he got thirsty and swallowed some snow, which gave him a stomach cramp, and he had to withdraw. Cross-country is murder anyway: you need the mentality of a watchmaker, since you've nothing to compete against except time.

With jumping he had more success. He had worked out a very individual take-off, a sort of leap from the crouch position such as people used to do on the old looping boards, which slope upwards at the tip. Nowadays the take-off board is built with a slight downward slant, which allows the jumper to maintain his speed as he sweeps over the tip, jerking from the hips and bringing up the skis on straight legs. It needs a lot of practice, since at the moment of take-off the body involuntarily tenses, and the instinct is to draw in one's legs. That's exactly how Zwiesel jumped, drawing a wide curve in the air and flailing about until he had regained balance and could make some sort of landing. Frequently he would flap his arms in vain, lying crosswise or in an extreme forward position. There would be screams from the onlookers, who usually began to scream anyway when he took off in that vilely unsportsmanlike backwards crouch position of his. They would hear him shouting curses at the wind as he swept down the steep final run. After once breaking a thumb at it, he went back to downhill skiing.

At that period Harlacher was for keeping Zwiesel out of the competition. He wanted only first-class men. Dolterer had argued with him, pointing out that Zwiesel often produced surprises and could, when his luck was with him, beat all the favorites. But Harlacher replied, not unreasonably, that the favorites ought to win, otherwise the spectators would be disappointed. Ranzonso lived on its winter sports, after all, and was only one of many resorts, and did not have the advantage of being either in Switzerland or near a big city.

"You're skiing for Ranzonso and not to satisfy your own ambitions," Harlacher said. "And for that you get a couple of free weeks living on our money. And what's more we pay your fares both ways. We live one for the other. Nobody gives you a thought in the summer, when you're working in some sports shop selling air mattresses and bathing shoes. If you're in the competitions you're expected to be fast and technically expert. That'll last for ten years at the very most, and then maybe you can get a ski instructor's job or open up a boardinghouse. Ranzonso will even sell you a building plot at a reduced price."

On the morning of the race Dolterer did not go out alone for track practice but took Zwiesel with him.

"Why should I come?" Zwiesel grumbled. "I promised some fellows in the dairy to play cards with them."

"You must get a more fluid style, or you won't be allowed to start."

"Of course I'll start. I've done the Beluga three times already. I know every mogul on it."

"You don't know a damn thing," Dolterer shouted at him. "The gully by the yew tree is a sheet of ice, the track through the woods has a large patch with no snow at all which you've got to jump, and on the run from the north curve there's wet snow, and the moguls look different every day. You've got to swing out farther down, or it'll throw you into the trees."

"I don't want to know that much about it," Zwiesel said. "Once I start to think I can't move at all."

However, Dolterer would not relent. He dragged him to the lift and took him up the Beluga. At the top station Zwiesel suddenly said he wasn't feeling well. Dolterer got him a couple of schnapps. Then the toe clamps on the footplate of his skis turned out to be loose. Dolterer got a screw driver from the lift hut and tightened the clamps, while Zwiesel stood beside him trying to think up new excuses. But before he found anything Dolterer said, "You might as well give up racing right away, you stupid railroader. If you're not prepared to learn, you'll find yourself shunting cars in Dornbirn in the winter too."

"So I'm just a railroader, am I?"

Dolterer did not want to quarrel. All he wanted was to show Zwiesel how to traverse the first slope, where the gradient is so steep that one can scarcely get in a turn. The only way is to cut with the steel edges diagonally through the opposite slope before the ice gully, so as to keep clear of the woods and hit the upper track at the right point.

"Hold your hat and grab your poles," Zwiesel said. In a single wild spurt he got slightly in front, then turned around right in the middle of the steep slope to see if Dolterer was coming. Without falling. And when Dolterer came to a halt Zwiesel threw himself down, since he could not remain upright on the narrow rib of snow between the rocks below the starting gate.

"Come on," he shouted, "come on, or I'll break your neck!"

In a series of little tailor-made hops Dolterer picked his way down the strip of snow to Zwiesel, taking up an extreme forward position, absorbing the extra weight each time in his knees and transforming it into the succeeding jump like a dancing grasshopper. With a final jump turn between the poles he came up beside Zwiesel.

"With a bit of technique you could make mincemeat of us all," Dolterer said.

"I'll make mincemeat of you anyway."

"Be sensible."

"What do you expect from a railroader?" Zwiesel said.

They both got to their feet. Since there was no room to stand on the steep and narrow ledge, they set off together, Dolterer in a close crouch position, Zwiesel leaning stiffly backwards.

Side by side they clattered down the frozen slope. There was no time for turning. Each had to aim for the entry to the track and try before the other to take the left curve across the icy gully, which at that terrific speed two could not traverse together. Zwiesel, being the heavier, was the first to move to the left, forcing Dolterer, who was half a ski length behind, over to the side. With a wild jump to the right behind Zwiesel he managed to get himself clear. He saw Zwiesel with murderous speed shoot vertically down into the gully, while he himself was obliged to level off on the opposite slope and slide along the top edge with the velocity of a bobsled toward the snow saddle and its surface of mirrorlike ice. There they drew nearer to each other again. Zwiesel jumped, Dolterer at once followed suit, and one behind the other they shot off down the narrow track.

"Look out!" Dolterer howled. "Mud!" For there was hardly any snow on the middle stretch of the track.

Dolterer could see people waving spades at them. As Zwiesel began to wobble, he bore to the right as far as he could, so as to get past if Zwiesel fell. He swept over a mogul, jumped, slapped down on the next mogul and jumped again, drawing from his velocity a taut elastic rhythm. His speed increased, metal and distorted faces flashed past him, reminding him all of a sudden that the course was officially closed on the day of the race. He jumped again, throwing himself from one ridge to the other, with ever gathering speed. Once again he caught up with Zwiesel, who was running along beside the trees far over to the left —less running than staggering, since there were patches of new snow covering up the roughnesses.

"I'm coming!" Dolterer called out, then yelled, "Look out!" But Zwiesel could not move aside, and he had to pull out to the right and get in position for the turn on the bend in the north slope. Dolterer realized that at the very moment when, just ahead of Zwiesel, he swept across the last rise. Anger shot through him as his skis began to flutter. Exerting all his strength, he kept himself upright, did a couple of skips, and then was borne struggling over the north curve, which had to be taken at an angle against the impetus, otherwise the velocity hurls one into the fir plantation. Dolterer managed it, and felt safe again as he reached the large hollow, a steep but even stretch of the course, from which, almost at right angles, one entered the Cannonbarrel, another narrow trail leading out in the final straight.

The hollow was relatively easy to negotiate. It was the fastest section of the course, and speeds up to sixty miles an hour were not uncommon there. Dolterer ran straight down the middle, pressing his poles to his sides with his elbows and pumping with the upper part of his body, a way of increasing speed by juggling with the center of gravity. He wanted to get to the Cannonbarrel ahead of Zwiesel in order to avoid a serious crash.

Cautiously he began to traverse in an effort to reduce speed and get into position for the entry to the narrow trail. And then he saw Zwiesel, who had taken the hollow along the top to the left corner. The madman stood for an instant poised on the extreme edge and then slid off to his left straight down the fall line to the Cannonbarrel. Dolterer crouched down for his turn, but already Zwiesel, arms outstretched to maintain balance, had swished past a little lower down. He hunched himself up and dived in between the trees. Then Dolterer was also in the Cannonbarrel.

There they could only let their skis ride and take care that the frozen ridges should not knock them off course. One behind the other they shot down the path. If Zwiesel could have heard, Dolterer would have shouted to him. His whole attention concentrated on the trail ahead, he let the trees flash by to either side, tensed himself for the jolt he knew would come when he shot from the Cannonbarrel into wet snow over which, by aiming for a particular hump, he could leap. He summoned all his strength.

In front of him Zwiesel was struggling, getting faster and faster and more desperate, yet always regaining control and riding the moguls. Then maybe Dolterer let out a cry now, anyway he was suddenly breathless. He stuck out his right shoulder, shaved the final tree as close as a slalom pole, jumped, and saw Zwiesel on his left shoot twisting up into the air. With an immense effort he did a series of braking turns and at last managed to bring himself to a standstill far down the slope. Panting, he turned to look at Zwiesel, who lay on the snow above him, motionless.

Zwiesel never regained consciousness. His skull had been fractured, a piece from his splintered ski poles had pierced his throat, a branch sticking up through the snow had torn open his liver. In the afternoon race Dolterer came third. An American won it. By that time his friend Zwiesel was already dead. Spills like that can always happen on runs as fast as the Beluga.

"There's corn snow on the slopes, and the forest tracks are icy," Maschlings said. "I shall wear a crash helmet. Rapponard knocked up his elbows yesterday."

"You go and put in some practice," said Dolterer, "and leave me sitting here."

"I'll get warmed up at the top station. The course is closed now."

Dolterer could not stand the buffet any longer. He went out, but not until he had promised Maschlings to be back in an hour.

Nobody was allowed now on the final run, but outside the ropes hordes of skiers were showing in varying degrees of speed what they could do, giving the spectators a foretaste of the race to come. A sunny, tingling day such as it had turned out to be encourages even beginners to deeds of daring.

Dolterer kept well to one side. Skiers were approaching from all directions, putting on their skis carefully when they reached the lift. It took a full ten minutes with long thongs. The men gathered in groups around their trainers, arguing, laughing, talking loudly so that the onlookers would know they were contestants: they were given their numbers only when they were at the starting point. The ladies arrived singly, with preoccupied faces. Dolterer would dearly have liked to join in, but he was afraid he might do badly. He would not mind being the noncompetitive opener, throwing the course open and at the same time turning in a time very few could equal.

More ladies came up, a whole swarm of them. Judging from their dress they were local girls, and on their home ground they would probably outrun all the foreign ladies. Dolterer watched them closely. He saw the Burgel girl, who had moved right up in the rankings last year; Senta Moser, with her beefy upper arms; then the pretty Catapucci girl, who was married to a Viennese doctor: he had seen a picture in the newspaper. There were the Rieder sisters, who looked almost like twins and frequently finished close together. Dolterer began to fidget. He waited, but Monika did not come.

It was a truly beautiful winter's day, with plenty of sun and a mild breeze which seemed to bring the mountains nearer. Dolterer stamped on the snow, but unostentatiously, with lowered head, so that the skiers would not see who he was. He began again to think about his examination. Finally he went back to his car, which was parked near the travel bureau, and seated himself in it.

After his graduation from high school—his marks had been satisfactory—his father had had a brain wave: he should become a teacher. He had never shown any interest in mechanics, and the family as a whole had no business sense, so that left only government service. It was safe, after all, and was the logical extension in academic terms of his father's administrative career: he had begun as a clerk in the Kaufbeuren town hall and would probably end up in the Munich Archives.

During his first three terms at the university Dolterer had gone on racing. Then he gave it up for lack of proper training. In contrast to his school, which had been very tolerant of his sporting ambitions, the university was completely indifferent to his reputation as a consistently good skier. The Ski Club had offered him aid and had advised him to aim at the managerial side. However, his studies took up so much time that he had to refuse. He took pleasure in giving to his studies the same meticulous attention that he had formerly lavished on his sports training.

Two years previously in the autumn he had paid a visit to
Monika Harlacher. She had started skiing on the Beluga when
she was sixteen and had been quite good. Later she had been
taken in hand by the best instructors in Ranzern and had developed into a slalom expert. He had met her at various competitions. Then he heard that she was attending the drama
school in Munich. He was surprised, for she had never told him
that her interests lay in that direction. He visited her in Munich
of course, and they had got to know each other better. Her father was against her choice of profession, and so she had had to
accept an engagement before her final examination in order to
earn money.

From Munich Dolterer drove on his motor scooter to Mengsfeld, near Bad Ochs, where Monika was appearing. It was
nearly two hundred miles, and the scooter was old. It rained almost the whole way, and he felt stiff and cramped when he at
last reached Mengsfeld, a village set in a landscape of hills and
empty fields. He saw one or two hunting lookouts, but otherwise nothing.

In the village he learned that the theater was in the villa, a
heavy brick pile with a moss-covered roof and fir trees in front,
which he discovered on the outskirts. In the courtyard there was
a white-haired man, whom he asked where Monika was to be
found. Going on, he realized suddenly that the man had not
been wearing a hat, in spite of the rain. He turned his head to
look. The man was watching him too. Dolterer went quickly
into the house. The upstairs corridor had a large number of
doors and, not knowing where to go, he called out Monika's
name. She appeared immediately at the door before which he
happened to be standing, pale, thin, and red-haired.

She was overjoyed to see him, asked at once whether he had
any cigarettes with him, and offered him a seat on her bed. At
last Dolterer was able to slip out of his wet coat. Monika's small
room was in the attic. There was no chair as far as he could see,
and everything was in a state of chaos—clothes, shoes, books,
and even underwear lying about on the floor. However, as Dol-

terer reminded himself, the artistic life was bound to bring big changes.

"We're playing in Schweinfurt tonight," she said. "We leave here at four. Will you come? Then you can see me act."

"Of course," he said. "But don't you play here?"

"Only twice a month. There aren't enough people. We go off to other places—twenty-five of them—leaving here in the afternoons and coming back at night. Then at about eleven or twelve next day we start rehearsing again. Sometimes we're not back until two in the morning, when we've been to Kreutern or Bissen. According to union rules we should have at least ten hours free. But you must be loyal: the management does what it can."

"Do you enjoy it?"

"I took over from a girl who had a baby unexpectedly."

"Unexpectedly?"

"Most of us here are on short contract, except for a few of the older ones who have got stuck. I suppose she thought no one would notice, but she was already in her fifth month when she came. So now I've taken over."

"Shall we go out for a bit?" he said.

"Can we go to Bad Ochs on your scooter? It's weeks since I've been anywhere really. We just rehearse, sit in a bus, play in a gym, and then get back in the bus. I could do with a change."

They had to leave at once if they were to be back in time. Dolterer questioned her about her colleagues, interested to know what life was like in the theater. Monika told him that, being always together, they were delighted when they didn't see each other for a few hours at a stretch. Some had homes in the village, but most of them—the young ones, who were in the majority—had rooms in the villa, for which they paid fifty marks a month.

"I earn only two hundred and thirty," she said, "and make-up alone takes thirty of that. You can't really live on it. The food in the restaurant is atrocious and a meal costs two marks. Then you need something for the bus, because you're tired and have to eat to keep awake. I ought to have more clothes than I have. For modern plays we have to provide our own, only costumes for the historical ones are supplied. And it's all horrible stuff—smelly and shabby. We got much better things in Ranzonso for the carnival procession."

"Don't you still ski?" Dolterer asked.

"Don't talk to me about that. I'm an actress now, as you'll be seeing today. It's not much of a part, but I'm learning a lot. You have to be able to play anything here. All the great actors started their careers in the provinces, you know. For instance, we're doing a musical next, and I've got to learn tap-dancing, because I play a once-famous dancer who drives all the gold-diggers crazy. It's really quite a play. Our scenic designer is teaching me to tap-dance: he was a choreographer once in a theater in Thuringia."

Bad Ochs is not far from Mengsfeld, and in a quarter of an hour they were there. Seated on the scooter behind him, Monika yodeled for joy and on the curves leaned over so far that Dolterer once almost ran off the road.

They went for a meal first: fish with a thick sauce, and pineapple. Then Monika decided to buy something, but could not make up her mind what. Dolterer, who did not have much money, bought her a necklace of red wooden beads to prevent her choosing something he could not afford. She was delighted, thanked him profusely, put it on at once, and, as they walked on, clung tightly to his arm.

They had meant to take a walk in the park, but the heavy rain had made the paths soft and muddy. They went to the café in the Casino, which was still open, and sat down. The few other guests all looked like locals—not surprisingly, since the season was over and most of the hotels were closed. Dolterer remarked that anybody could take the cure these days, since it was all paid for by medical insurance. She sat there drinking coffee and smoking one cigarette after another.

Then it was time to go back to Mengsfeld, where the bus was waiting. Since Dolterer's scooter was slower than the bus, he started off for Schweinfurt right away. It was a good sixty miles, and he was relieved that the rain had stopped. Somewhere along the road a bus passed him which he thought was the theater one. Monika had not waved, but in any case it was too dark.

In Schweinfurt he saw her for the first time on the stage. Though he was tired after all the driving he had done, he was very much impressed. She came on after the intermission. It was a French comedy, and she played the daughter who steals her mother's lover. She was really excellent. To Dolterer she seemed another person entirely. He joined vigorously in the applause at the end. Afterwards he waited a long time outside the theater, but Monika did not appear. He did not dare go back in, though there were some doors at the side, one of which must have led backstage. But he was not sure he could find his way to her. All the other actors would probably still be in their dressing rooms, and he did not know any of them. He debated whether to drive back to Mengsfeld. But Monika would be in bed by the time he got there. In the end he took a room in Schweinfurt for the night. He slept very badly, for his weak stomach began to plague him again. Next morning he drove the two hundred and fifty miles straight back to Munich.

A year later he heard that Monika had given up the stage and was now living in Amsterdam with a musician. He was told she wasn't doing too well. Then someone said she was in Spain with another man, an Englishman. One of his skiing companions in Munich even claimed to have spent the night with her once.

There was a sudden thunderclap on the window of his car. Kalb and Rapponard were standing outside.

"Come on," they shouted. "We're going up to the start: it's almost time for the race. Harlacher is up there already."

Dolterer leaped out of the car. "I'll make mincemeat of you all," he cried. "I'll mow down everyone and everything that gets in my way!"

"That's the spirit!" they cheered. "Babe Dolterer's daring us. Come on, we must get moving."

"Daring you?" Dolterer said. "I shall ski straight down the fall line. The clocks won't be able to keep up with me."

He got his skis, poles, and boots from the cellar of the buffet and put them on while Rapponard and Kalb were talking to the man at the lift. Only competitors were supposed to use it so close to the start.

The man remembered Dolterer. "If it was up to me," he said, "all the bloody competitors could walk up. That's how it was in my day, when alpine sport really was sport."

"Oh, shut up," said Dolterer. He snatched the supporting bar from the liftman's hand, tucked it under his bottom, and was hauled off upwards. Rapponard and Kalb were hooked on in front of him; Maschlings, he supposed, was already at the top.

Dolterer watched the course closely, mapping out for himself the best descent line through the various humps and ridges. He took note of the positions of the slalom poles put up in order to force the skiers to turn at dangerous corners. In his mind's eye he saw the two tracks leading through the woods: they would be icy, as they always were, with moguls and washboards and patches of thin snow. On the open slopes like the hollow and the north curve there was a fast corn snow, which had frozen in the night and thawed out during the day. His skis had exactly the right running surface for that, a layer of hard varnish over woven fabric. A bit of graphite would give his first spurt down the steep slope below the starting point even more speed. He felt light-headed with eagerness and excitement as they reached the top.

It took them quite a time to find Harlacher. He was standing in a group of timekeepers and trainers, who were all busy complaining about things that Harlacher was no longer in a position to change. Before the start of a race officials always grumble about everything: the weather, the difficulty or easiness of the course, the electric timing gear, the jury, the prize distribution. Competitors and spectators were moving about between them, the first warming themselves up and checking the fit of skis and boots, the spectators aping them.

Rapponard pushed his way through, calling as he went, "Herr Harlacher, Dolterer's here and he wants to compete."

Harlacher did not hear him at first. He was deep in argument with the president of a Swiss club, who claimed that three of the Austrian competitors were pros who had appeared in advertising films for a ski factory. Harlacher was quite unmoved. For all he cared, his respected colleague or his grandmother for that matter could go and make advertising films too. The winter was over and the race was strictly friendly.

"FIS," the Swiss gentleman said beseechingly. "What about the FIS rules?"

Harlacher at last caught sight of Dolterer standing in front of him. "What are you doing here?" he asked. "I thought you were studying."

"I want to join in," Dolterer said.

"You're not entered."

"I know that, but perhaps I could do the opening run."

"Pepi Weingarten is doing the opening run."

"But he's got an artificial leg."

"That's why he's doing the opening run," Harlacher said. "Don't kid yourself. Pepi is faster than you anyway."

"He is not," said Dolterer, his temper rising. Then without thinking he went on, "I never touched her. It wasn't my fault."

Harlacher put out a hand and drew him a few steps off to the side. "Where is she?" he asked. "Is she in Amsterdam?"

"No, she's in Spain, isn't she?"

"In Spain?"

"So I was told a couple of years ago."

"A couple of years," Harlacher said. "Weren't you with her at all?"

"Only a very short time."

"Was she in a play?"

"Yes. But not in Munich. Somewhere in Franconia."

"You saw it? How was she?"

"She was splendid," Dolterer said. "I never thought she had it in her."

"That's all right then," Harlacher said and nodded. "And you want to compete, do you? But what can I do? I've got far too many already. It's only a three-minute run and there're sixty-one entries. I could let them go at one-minute intervals, I suppose, but what if somebody falls? They'll run into each other. If you want to wait five hours, I can put you in at the end."

"I'd prefer to do the opening run," Dolterer said.

"That's Weingarten's. I promised it to him. And what better opener could I have anyway than the first Beluga champion of thirty years ago? Particularly as he's got an artificial leg."

"I'm not going to be the last," Dolterer said.

"Suit yourself," Harlacher said, and walked away.

Wearing his heavy racing skis, without skins or braking wax, Dolterer set off up the slope behind the lift, herringboning at first, then, as he got winded, doing shaky kick turns, slithering and leaning heavily on his poles. He did not turn until he reached the rocks. From there he could see little splinters detaching themselves one after another from the dark mass, sliding off down the slope and vanishing into the woods by the hollow. Dolterer turned his eyes back upwards to focus on the flank above the rocks. The sun had already thawed the corn snow in patches, and there were no snow pennants over the peak. He decided to take off his skis and do the last part on foot. At this time of year there was no danger of avalanches.

Saturday in Nüssen

The factory is closed on Saturdays. But I usually go in to the office in the morning to prepare the orders for Monday. We make furniture, but not in a large way, so we have to be a bit quicker off the mark than the others—particularly when my uncle is at the trade fair getting as many orders as possible for the autumn. In a family concern like ours you always have to work hard and set an example. It's no good saying it's got nothing to do with you. Not that I mind—in a one-horse town like Nüssen there's nothing much else to do anyway. Besides, I stand to get a partnership in the factory myself eventually. When that happens, I intend to change over to standard kitchens. It's the big lines that really matter—not, as my uncle maintains, the special orders. As a small firm with a long-standing reputation, he says, we can never hope to compete with the modern firms. I think he's wrong: there's always a market for cheap aluminum kitchens.

Karli rang shortly after eleven, Heiner a little later, and we arranged to meet at two o'clock at the lake for a swim. The Maisee is never overcrowded, and the Reutles would certainly be there. They've got a chalet right beside the water with a dock, which is useful, because the lake is rather shallow and elsewhere you have to wade through reeds and mud before it's deep enough to swim.

Georg Reutle and I were together in elementary school, then he went on to the secondary modern while I was sent to a boarding school. He is Catholic and I'm a Protestant. I'm not such close friends with him as I am with Heiner or Karli, though Karli has been in Nüssen only two years, and Heiner is five years older. However, when you're in your thirties such differences hardly matter.

Heiner runs a pharmacy. He's a biologist really, studied at Freiburg and used to work in the research department of a pharmaceutical company. Not because he was particularly ambitious, but simply because he's patient and was quite happy preparing one bacteria culture after another. Then his father died, and he had to take over the pharmacy. There were two sisters to be taken care of, so the family didn't want to sell. If it had been me, I should have talked my mother into selling and stayed with the pharmaceutical company. That way each of them would have had a nice little bit of capital. Now he has to sweat his guts out so he can buy his sisters out when they want to get married. His shop does well and he has put in a new photographic department, but all the same it irks him not to be working as a scientist.

Karli works with Posselt, the dentist. Posselt's wife, who had been a dentist too, died of leukemia just as their new house in Wangener Strasse was ready for occupation. In a joint practice they had done very nicely, but Posselt couldn't manage to pay off his expensive new house all on his own, and had to engage an assistant. So Karli came, and people soon got used to him. The practice is flourishing and the house will soon be paid for, but Karli is certain he will be kept on. The point is that Posselt has a marriageable daughter who plays the organ in St. Paul's Church. Karli heads the list of possible husbands, being already in the practice and so in a position to take over in time. Not unnaturally, he intends to make the most of his advantages while he can. Posselt often sends him off in the middle of the afternoon to the tennis courts in an effort to make life in Nüssen attractive. Karli fulfills his part of the bargain by deploying his charm on daughter Ruth. He could take her any time he wants, he says, but he holds back in case he ever gets sick of Nüssen and needs an excuse to be thrown out. Ruth is now only nineteen, and she takes her organ-playing very seriously. It sends shivers down my spine whenever I hear her playing the old masters in St. Paul's. There must be a lot of satisfaction in it for her, I feel, and the charm of a young dentist is not much to put up against it. But it works out quite well, for Karli too. The girl doesn't see what is going on, and so he can please himself as to how long he stays on in his comfortable position. And since Papa Posselt has got his plans for the future as firmly fixed in his mind as he had his house building earlier, he's not even aware that his daughter has no thoughts for Karli.

It had now got so hot that I lost all appetite for work. I drove off home. There are three of us in the house: my mother, my grandmother, and myself. My father has been missing since the war. When my grandfather died some years ago we sold his house and took Granny in with us. It works quite well and has given my widowed mother a new purpose in life, now I'm grown up, looking after the old woman.

I started off for the lake immediately after lunch. The other two wouldn't be there yet: Heiner doesn't shut up shop till two on Saturdays, and Karli usually gets a few stragglers under his drill.

It's a lovely drive out to the Maisee. As far as landscape goes I've nothing against Nüssen. It's on the extreme edge of the Württemberg Allgäu district, and you get a very good view of the Alps, since the mountains around there are not more than three thousand feet. These are the celebrated Allgäu *Grasberge*, which can be treacherous enough in wet weather. It's easy to slip and, if you do, there's nowhere to catch hold. Every year we get a few deaths, since inexperienced visitors imagine it's safe to climb these grassy slopes in ordinary walking shoes. We have the advantage of the big ten and twelve thousanders without having to huddle under great threatening masses of stone as they do in Oberstdorf and Riezlern. And we can reach them easily enough when we want to. An hour's drive brings us to the high mountains or to Lake Constance or Austria or Switzerland. It's all at our doorstep. That's what I always tell myself when I'm driving through the Allgäu: Nüssen may be a small town, but the countryside is lovely.

Phrosine was at the chalet with her two children. There was another car standing beside hers, and it was not her husband's.

Phrosine has always got some bachelor or other in tow, and no one ever knows who is the man of the moment. With her you can never be sure in any case, but it's generally assumed that something is going on with one of them at least. She is a plump little thing, and has to take care she doesn't run to fat before her time. She turned up in Nüssen quite suddenly with a child. Georg is a lucky man to have her, for she keeps him on his toes. When he comes home all in after a day spent visiting his four-teen or fifteen dairies, she nags him until he invites someone to come along. And what does a man do then, when he is on the heavy side and is tired and doesn't care for dancing? He drinks himself silly and puts on a bit more weight. Then we carry him up to bed and go on dancing with Phrosine.

The second car belonged to the young curate of St. Mary's. He was sitting in a deck chair behind the bushes, playing with the children. Invariably, whether he's swimming, sailing, or playing tennis, he wears the same pair of white shorts. I suppose it's only because he's a curate that they always seem so very short. Phrosine was out on the dock, sunbathing. I got un-dressed and went over to her. To look at, she's really like all girls in the middle twenties. The two children have made no differ-ence. Georg's dairies, the new house, a car of her own, a chalet on the Maisee and for the past year a part share in a ski lift in Oberstdorf—these things have given her confidence. She's a married woman, and people know her. It wouldn't surprise me in the least if she hadn't always been as pretty as she is now.

She did not feel like going into the water, she said, she was too comfortable where she was. And she rolled from side to side on her beach towel. It looked both funny and alluring.

"Where's your husband?" I asked.

"He's gone to an association meeting in Dorenwaid. They want to start a new dairy, and he needs all the milk he can get. We're building a cheese factory."

"So I've heard. Everything fully automatic. You pour in milk at one end and out come ready-wrapped cheese slices at the other."

"The very latest thing."

"And you get left on your own."

"Never mind—the weather's fine."

"And I suppose the children keep you busy."

She laughed. "That's what the curate's for," she said. He came often. He was very open-minded, and you could say what you liked in front of him, but you couldn't sunbathe in the nude. Maybe that was what she really wanted to do. Anyway, I took it as an invitation and began to stroke her back. In the process she nearly fell off the dock, and I had to hold her tight. But there was nothing more in it than that. And in any case a couple of collapsible boats were passing by close in at the time. Still, with a married woman you can often do more in public than you can when you're alone together. Nobody thinks there can be anything behind it: it just looks harmless and silly.

Then I went in for a swim. Floating around on my back, I thought again how lovely our countryside really is, with its green hills, blue skies, dark woods, and scattered farms. People were busy loading up hay in the fields, and along the road two cars were raising clouds of dust.

That was Heiner and Karli. I watched them turn off down the path through the fields and come to a stop near the chalet. Karli came down so hard on his brakes that the car skidded on the gravel. Now we could get started. I swam back to the dock.

We sat on the veranda in front of the chalet, drinking beer. Phrosine was still in her bathing things and so were we. The curate, sitting over by the bushes with the children, waved to us. Phrosine was safe on all sides: she could take a light from Heiner, leaning toward him and supporting herself with a hand on his bare thigh, and Karli could make silly remarks, but nothing would come of it. Pleasantly warm, we could all sit there drinking beer, gazing at Phrosine's bare flesh and telling ourselves nothing was happening. As of course it wasn't. I decided that today I would make something happen. That is after all what Saturdays are for, after a week spent working hard.

"Have none of you got a girl?" Phrosine asked. "You, Heiner?"

"Nothing steady," Karli said.

"We're the most eligible bachelors in Nüssen," Heiner said

with a laugh. "So we have to watch out. Now we are free to take our pick." He patted Phrosine's arm. "But if it's a question of marriage, one's got to think carefully and long."

"*You* certainly must," I said. "You need one who'll bring as much into the business as your two sisters will one day take out."

"My sisters are not at all bad. Which one will you have?"

"In two years from now Mäusle, if she doesn't get any fatter."

"Mäusle!" Karli cried. "I don't see any difference except that Mäusle still tucks her skirt up when she goes riding on her bike."

"You men," Phrosine said. "I'm going to go join the curate."

"He's got an eye on Mäusle too," said Karli.

"Not so loud—he's a good boy, watching my children." Phrosine can blush when her husband's not around.

I reminded Karli that it was almost time for the football game. That made him sit up, as I knew it would, for there is nothing he likes better on a sunny afternoon by the water than to sit in a room watching television. And sure enough, he went off inside and was soon shouting goal and foul.

"And now if Heiner goes off for a swim I shall be even happier," I ventured again.

"Why should he if he doesn't want to?" Phrosine said. "Leave him alone."

But Heiner took me up. "I'll go and talk to the curate and see he doesn't look."

And with that he went off, which wasn't really what I had been intending. I had only meant it as a joke to find out if Phrosine would be embarrassed.

"What happens now?" she asked.

"Nothing."

I suppose I was looking at her rather stupidly

"What's the matter? Anything wrong? Why send everyone away? Now look, you're on the wrong track—that won't work with me. I know what they all say back in the town. They're just jealous because I don't come from here. It's just the same in Wangen. So skip it. I'm not all that stupid, I don't do things that way—and least of all with any of your crowd. You're not all that irresistible."

"Keep your shirt on," I said. "I know my ears are too big, but you can't deny that Karli has charm."

"Karli and his charm! I never hear the end of it. And what else has he got to offer? Maybe I have less charm—what of it? I know how you make fun of Georg behind his back, don't think I don't. But that doesn't make you stop drinking his whisky."

"We've got nothing against Georg."

"Very well then, you haven't. Why should you? In our house you can shout your heads off and smash all the glasses. But you try that on someone else and see where you get."

Her voice was getting louder and louder, and the football game was drawing to an end inside the chalet. "Phrosine," I implored her, "it was only a joke. I just said the first thing that came into my head."

"Why do you make fun of me? I know why—because it's easy, because I play along with you. All Georg's friends can paw me and mess me around, because it doesn't look bad when I'm married to Georg. It's never serious because it can't be. Why don't you go and try it on other girls? Because you haven't the guts—it's simpler just to mess around a bit with me. You know I won't take it seriously. It's all quite safe and gives you something to gossip about."

She started to cry. Never had I expected to see Phrosine sitting on her veranda bawling like a baby. Karli came rushing out. "Phrosine, Phrosine—what's the matter with my little Phrosine?"

She shrieked at him to get out: she never wanted to see any of us again. I didn't know what else to do. Karli walked with me to the dock. We beckoned to Heiner, who was still swimming, and then we all of us got dressed. I told them everything that had happened. I hadn't really meant it in the least seriously, and neither had Heiner, who had only been playing along, as we always play along with Phrosine. In fact we thought the playing was rather on her side.

"The day's young yet," Karli said. "Let's go somewhere else. Maybe Phrosine just has her period."

We got into our cars and drove off one behind the other toward Lindau. We took the route we know so well, more circuitous than the main road through the mountains, along a succession of dirt roads tipping down through gorges and up through the woods, and suddenly you come on cows in the middle of the road or occasionally tractors pulling carts piled with hay. We drove along with our bumpers almost touching. There are blind corners and the sand is skiddy, but steer into them, the spokes of the wheel gripped tight in the hand, feet busy on the pedals, slip into gear while still giving it the gas, and you're through. Anyone anxious to pass won't get by unless he grazes the grass at the edge with his offside wheels, and usually by then he's on the next bend, where there's not room for two. On the last half-dozen miles to the lake we use the tarred main road for a final spurt. It's great fun, particularly on Saturdays, when the tourists are out in droves and you have to nip from one gap to the next between them.

We always carry ties with us just in case, for in Lindau you are not allowed into the Casino without one. The room to the left is for roulette and the glass veranda to the right for tea and dancing. In the summer the town is packed tight, and there's never a spare seat in the three cafés down by the harbor. The motorboats are booked up by water-skiers for days ahead. That's why we usually make straight for the Casino: on sunny afternoons the crush is not so great.

Heiner knows one of the waiters in the restaurant. He took us to a table at which two girls—secretary or student types—were already sitting. After a couple of dances we had them tagged. They were salesgirls in a shoeshop in Bruchsal and were having a week's holiday. They were not bad—well dressed, good hairdos, good figures. I liked the taller one especially, with her thighs nicely defined beneath a plain skirt. But then the old

Saturday afternoon problems start to arise: what's the best way of getting off with a girl? How do you bring her to the point? Where and when—now or later in the evening? And is it best to start with the drinks right away?

It's simpler as a rule with the country types. You dance, make a grab, and drive out to the woods. There you get either a punch in the nose or what you're after. But you know pretty well which it will be even before you get into the car.

With town girls on holiday things are more complicated. These two had almost for a certainty come to the Casino in search of someone classy with a car or a motorboat. Worse than that, it was only their second day in Lindau, so they'd probably not yet be in the giving mood, but would be trying for the motorboat over the whole week. When one of them went off to the ladies' room Heiner took the other out onto the dance floor, and Karli and I went into conference. There was only one chance as far as we could see, and that was to play roulette with them, have a few drinks, and somehow or other get ourselves into their boardinghouse before supper, so they wouldn't get suspicious. It was important that all three of us should go along with them, or they would start being coy. We must make the whole thing look like a friendly get-together. Then, when preferences were established, the odd man out would quietly vanish. It would be too much of a bore just to keep on dancing with them, take them out for a meal, then go on dancing while we waited for the evening to end. Then maybe, taking them home by a devious route, nothing might happen after all. And if it didn't work, the whole evening would be wasted. No, we must do the unexpected, be self-confident, always one step ahead. So we went gambling.

The gaming tables in the Lindau Casino are situated in a palm court, a vast plush grotto, glassed in on the lake side. My uncle's office, our showpiece for visitors, is done in the same style—what I call smoking-room baroque.

There was not much going on in the Casino. A few old hags were playing their systems, while a number of tourists looked respectfully on. The girls were eager to know how you set about winning, and I showed the bigger one all the things you can do: go for single numbers or for groups of numbers, odds or evens or colors, all of which are simple chances. I never do more than that, so as not to get out of my depth. Heiner took the other girl to a table. Karli bought himself ten five-mark counters, lost three of them at once by leaving them on the board, and then played against the bank. But it's no use preaching to Karli. When he loses he takes a personal grudge against the table and just crashes on, never varying his tactics, until he has lost the whole business. Heiner and I just play openly on simple chances, Heiner sometimes blind on two tables at once. There's not a lot to be got from it, but it's quite amusing.

The tall girl—her name was Irmgard—was nervous about starting. She was afraid of the croupiers, talking away in their rapid French. I placed for her—out of my own money, of course—and won. At the time there was a run on red, and I was right three times. I could have gone on for ten, but thought it better to get out early and be sure of a small profit rather than to lose the whole lot at once. Then Irmgard ventured something, and lost it. She tried again, but the table was erratic.

Heiner appeared at the other side of our table with his girl. He had a whole wad of blue five-mark counters in his hand.

"Where's Karli?" I asked him.

"Messing about somewhere with his last two counters."

"I've won twenty marks," his girl told us loudly. Some of the players looked up irritably at this desecration of the table's rustling solemnity. The wheel was already turning, was slowing down. Heiner's girl laid a bakelite counter uncertainly on the cloth, the croupier pushed it back with his rake, she snatched it awkwardly, and it fell on the floor. She bent down to retrieve it, but the head croupier, who sits on a sort of umpire's platform at the top of the table keeping an eye on things through his sunglasses, rang his little bell. "A counter fallen," he called.

The room attendant came along in his gold-braided jacket, wormed his way politely through the spectators, retrieved the fallen counter, and handed it over to Heiner's girl. She got red in the face, said it belonged to her companion and not to her, and gave it back to him. The attendant offered it to Heiner.

"Keep it," said Heiner magnanimously.

"*Merci* and *bonne chance*." The attendant pushed his way out.

Of course the girl was now flattened completely. She made a sign to Irmgard that it was time to go, but Irmgard, anxious not to draw attention to herself as well, had just placed a bet—forty marks' worth of my counters on number eighteen. A silly situation. If Heiner had now muffed it with the girls, I at any rate was going to get my money back. I put eighty marks on odd numbers.

Thirty-seven came up. I had won, and at the same time recouped Irmgard's lost forty.

Then the gambling fever seized me, in spite of the promise I had made my mother, after leaving more than a thousand marks behind in the Casino last spring, that I wouldn't do it again. I was dimly aware that Heiner had gone off with his girl and that Irmgard was no longer sitting beside me, but the ball was already rolling. I quickly covered two transversals and put eighty marks on evens. And won.

After four games I had three pink hundred counters lying in front of me. An elderly woman who was sitting near me begged me to come in on her system, but to suggestions of that sort I am deaf. I got up and offered my seat to a portly gentleman. You become sleepy sitting at a roulette table and keep on playing only because you're so comfortably close to it.

I passed up one game. Peering through the ring of spectators, I saw Heiner and Karli standing at the bar with the two girls, drinking. Good, I thought, they can get on with the job of softening the girls up, while I go on playing, at any rate till the first loss.

Somebody had shouldered me away from the table. I just had time to put another hundred on evens before "*Rien ne va plus*" was called. The ball clicked, hopped over the little brass knobs above the numbers on the inner side of the wheel, slowed down, spun, and came to rest on the six. An even number. I had won.

One of the croupiers paid out the winnings as the other raked in the losses. I waited as the counters flew back and forth. I always enjoy watching this operation. With a flick of the wrist the croupiers send the plastic disks sailing through the air in a lazy curve, to patter down on the cloth exactly in front of the winner.

As the simple chances came up for payment and an identical counter was put on each of the five *pair* wins, the players grabbed to pick them up, and some fellow put a large red paw over my two pink hundreds.

"Hey, those are mine," I said loudly.

But he had them in his hand now. Another bull-necked oaf dressed in a borrowed tie, who was standing beside him, replied in a ferocious accent, "Naw, none o' that—we won 'em."

The other people stopped talking to watch us.

"I put that hundred on *pair*."

"Anyone can say that," said this lout, who like his friend came from the other side of the lake—farmhands who came clumping through Lindau every Saturday to sin ostentatiously in the Casino because roulette is forbidden in their milk mountains back home.

"You've taken my counters," I protested. "Nobody but I put a pink hundred. Here, I've got another two in my pocket from my previous winnings. Are you claiming to have put a hundred?"

"Of course," they both insisted. "Those are our winnings, they belong to us. That's right, isn't it?" They turned to the croupier. "You were witness."

A croupier never takes part in a dispute. He leaves it all to the chief, whose job it is to keep a lookout. This one was now climbing cautiously down from his umpire's stand. Time passed as he went into a quiet huddle with his croupiers.

People began to whisper. I heard Karli's laugh and saw him standing with Heiner and the girls behind the ring of spectators. I could only see his head and the grin on his face.

And now at last the head croupier came slowly around the table. He looked pained as he adjusted his sunglasses and said, *"Les deux pièces sont à Monsieur."*

I pretended not to understand. I know the fellow, who rows stroke for the Lindau Boat Club and only puts on these airs when he is playing the grand panjandrum in the plush grotto.

"I don't understand you," I said loudly, ignoring the dairy lout beside me who was offering me the two pink disks.

"The counter and the winnings are yours. You have won. I saw you place your bet."

I put out a hand to receive the two sticky disks, then turned and went to the desk to change them. Behind me the ball had started clicking again, and the people were fluttering with excitement.

It will be a long time before the Casino sees me again. Of course Karli accused me right away of pinching both stake and winnings, but why should I have bothered to make myself interesting in front of the girls? They meant nothing to me now.

"Where are we going?"

"To eat," Heiner said. "Dachsler has won, so he can pay."

"I must go home to eat," I said. "My mother's expecting me."

"That's not true."

"It is if I say so."

"We must go too," the girl Irmgard said with a nod to her friend. She was still holding the twenty marks she had won in her hand. "Supper in the boardinghouse is at seven sharp."

"Can't we eat there too?" Heiner asked.

"No, we can't," I said. "A boardinghouse isn't a restaurant. But we'll drive the ladies there with pleasure." I went off toward the cloakroom, and at last the others caught on. While the girls were putting on their draperies I asked Heiner and Karli if there was still anything in it for us, but they also felt things were moving too slowly. You can't just lay the girls on the boardinghouse table.

So we took them off home, made a date with them for the beach on the following day, and roared off. We were feeling hungry and consequently in no mood for prolonged farewells.

We decided to eat in Oberstaufen, which lies to the north of Lindau at the edge of the Bregenzer Wald a half hour's drive away. It has a good restaurant high above a picture-postcard valley with cows and chalets, where the spa visitors on a slimming diet go when they get too famished.

After all the excitement in the Casino it was good to be sitting quietly together again. It's curious how, when one of us goes off on a job of his own, chasing a girl or something like that, defeat does not matter so long as we can get together afterwards and talk about it. Heiner in fact maintains that an affair is fun only when you can talk about it, and that's why he doesn't get married.

Karli, smarting from his fifty-mark loss, thawed out when the food came and he had made sure that I was going to pay for it. He thrust great lumps into his mouth, cutting a diagonal path through a heap of venison ragout and dumplings. With each movement of his fork he told us what he would have done with those Bruchsal broads—how he would have teased them, tempted them, shown them, denied them, given them, deprived them, hustled them, grabbed them. He knew exactly how to soften up birds of that sort: they had been ripe for it. But what could you do when Heiner mucked it up for us all with his grand manners? You couldn't show up inexperienced girls like that at a gaming table: they were very particular about their appearance in other people's eyes.

"And then they know no mercy," Karli concluded. "They close up like clams, for to their way of thinking getting on in society means keeping yourself buttoned up."

I had to laugh, but Heiner had not yet done with the subject. He took a noisy swig at his coffee.

"What else could I have done when she made such an ass of herself?" he asked.

"Did you want her or didn't you?" I asked.

"What do you mean—want? You take what you can get. But I wasn't all that keen."

"Him and keen," Karli said with a laugh. "All he really wants is me."

And now they both laughed. I don't much care for jokes of that sort. We've got a case of it in Nüssen, a young potter who goes off to the mountains every weekend on a motorcycle with his watchmaker friend.

"Dachsler's looking cross," Karli said. "He's much too healthy for such things. But joking aside, I'll tell you something that makes us all look like wet smacks. It concerns my boss, Nüssen's mighty toothpecker Posselt with house and organ-playing daughter. She makes the sixty-fourth sound like a rippling brook, but that's all the pleasure life now has to offer our little town mouse. When you've got no wife and have to spend your days drilling customers, I tell you, it's often damned difficult—especially on a hot day with a plump young chicken in the chair wearing next to nothing up top. Your eyes start to wander —down the neck and into the cleavage, reeking of nuts and eau de Cologne. When it's me, I peer through my mirror at their molars and shove in a clamp without any padding, so they have to keep their heads back or choke on their own saliva. Life is hard, as you see. And it's particularly hard on my boss, because he's small and doesn't want it known. So he winds the chair up too high—then he can look with his left eye into their mouths and lower down with his right.

"A fortnight ago he was more than usually edgy, not hav- ing been to Munich in weeks. He chased me all around and gave the laboratory assistant hell—we could do nothing right.

"I was finished by twelve, but he was still waiting for some- one. I thought it must be a private patient—he won't touch anything on Medicare after midday. I went off to the tennis courts, and an hour later he came steaming along for a singles with me. In a hell of a mood, too, smashing all his balls over the line or into the net. And then I suddenly saw Luitpold Sinz standing outside the cage—in the middle of his lunch break, when he normally only shuts up shop for half an hour so as not to miss any stray tractor driver who may come to town in search of rheumatism pills. He comes clumping across the court in his hand-sewn shoes, grinding his heels in the brick dust. And my boss, the President of the Tennis Club himself, just stands there holding his breath. 'Dr. Posselt, come with me please,' says Sinz loudly, then turns and goes back to his car. And my boss, gripping his tennis racquet tight and staring straight ahead, follows behind. Then they drive off."

"Sinz!" Heiner crowed, hopping about on his seat. "Open-air Sinz, who goes out hiking on the Krottenkopf every Sunday and is always copying my window display. If I put in a packet of herbs he retaliates with a string of garlic at least. Sinz, the nature worshiper, the barefoot wanderer in the morning dew, who keeps his kids in short pants right into November."

"But," I said, "he's building himself a new house too."

"So are all the other self-respecting citizens," said Heiner. "Take a look at the hill behind the cemetery. Butchers, bakers, and candlestick makers all buying up Siedberger's field as fast as they can. It'll be Nüssen's exclusive residential quarter before long."

"Are you jealous?" Karli asked.

"I don't give a damn about a house. The first thing is to get my shop window renovated, and that'll cost me a fortune. Sinz did up his shop last year, and what he can do I can do too. And just look at it. Pink! An architect from Stuttgart talked him into it. Eight thousand marks those interior decorations cost him—some sort of African wood."

"I like it," I said.

"Well, why not?" said Heiner. "But it's all just eyewash and it'll take him more than a couple of years to get it back. And then he grumbles because I'm selling headache pills too. But he'd better watch out: if necessary I'll take on a young chemist and open up a branch on the Felderholz estate. Refugees are our best customers—they can't get used to the climate."

"Heiner's getting all steamed up," Karli said. "He's a real businessman."

"And why not? My career's done for. If I've got to stick in Nüssen I might as well make money out of it. You'll come around to it yourself someday. You can't remain an assistant forever, can you? Just wait. I can see you in Mindelheim or some such Godforsaken joint with a bedroom, living room, and waiting room and a loan from the council to set up your office. And all the old dentists will be hopping mad because you've got the latest turbine drill and open shop at seven in the morning to catch a few extra typists coming in on the early train. You'll see, my boy. I know exactly how you'll finish up."

"You're quite wrong," Karli said. "I shall be dentist on a liner doing the Far East run. I shan't grow whiskers like you. I used to like tennis, but since I've been with Posselt I've come to hate it."

"Tennis!"

"Dachsler is getting fat on his miniature golf."

"It suits me."

It really doesn't worry me at all. And I'm not fat—just sturdily built. And anyway I do fifteen to twenty push-ups in the office every morning.

"So what happened between Posselt and Sinz?" I asked. "I need a drink."

We gave our orders and then Karli went on with his story. "Not a word against Sinz. He told me the whole business. And the rest you can work out for yourselves. The private patient after twelve o'clock for whom my boss was waiting was Frau Sinz."

"The skinny woman with the freckles?"

"That's it—Rabbit-face. She couldn't come at any other time because the assistant goes to lunch at one and she has to mind the shop. So she's all alone with Posselt: I'd gone off and the laboratory assistant was in her room at the back making a cast for Rapsmeier's dentures—that was a rush job because he was on counter duty at the bank that week."

"Get on with it."

"It was all strictly professional. Along comes the wife of a medical colleague by special arrangement and seats herself in the dentist's chair. Posselt pumps her up to the ceiling and squints into her mouth. She tells him it's the one with the gold crown that's hurting. Then, whether it was the fragrance wafting up from the rotten root, or whether it was the light summer dress she was wearing—anyway, my boss gets a sudden rush of blood to his head as he puts in the probe. He starts back, takes a deep breath, drops everything, and puts his hand down the opening of Frau Sinz's dress."

"But she hasn't got anything there."

"Perhaps he likes them skinny."

"She used to be a sprinter."

"All the same," Karli insisted, "he puts his hand there. Whether he found anything I couldn't say. Frau Sinz jumps up, slaps his face, and stalks off."

"With the gold crown?"

"Without the gold crown. She sent around for it a couple of days later and got our colleague Eggert to fix it again. But that's not the point. The interesting thing is that the two men involved didn't beat each other up. I'm on Sinz's side of course. I can't be for my boss. Nobody can be expected to back his boss, and anyway if I had been on his side Sinz wouldn't have told me about it."

"Just a moment. Why did Sinz tell you?" I was finding him difficult to follow.

Karli, who takes pride in being on intimate terms with everybody in Nüssen though he isn't a native, explained. "He had to tell somebody if he wanted his version of the hideous deed to get around. And I was his best bet. If it was left to my chief, then maybe it would have got around that Frau Sinz made a pass at him."

"Impossible," Heiner cried. "Sinz likes his oats too much."

"Nobody cares what really happened," said Karli, "only what they're told about it. As Posselt's assistant I was exactly the right person to tell, and after all I was playing tennis with him at the time. But really I'm against both parties. Posselt's roving hand was only the lead-in to an event of high political significance. But that was something Sinz didn't realize."

The drink and the talking had made Karli hungry again. He ordered a ham sandwich with pickled gherkins, and until it arrived sat in silence, though Heiner and I tried to provoke him into admitting that he had made it all up in order to score over us natives of Nüssen.

"Posselt and Sinz are people of education," Karli began again after he had finished his sandwich, "and both of them belong to the Free Voters League. The local elections are due in two months' time, and Posselt is a candidate. The Christian Union's candidate is Georg Reutle."

"What—Georg?"

"Yes, of course—Georg. You don't seem to have any idea who's out for power in Nüssen."

What did it matter anyway, Heiner asked: the new school and the gym were already complete and the cobbled roads had been tarred over only last year. The single remaining problem was whether the householders or the town should pay for the drains in the new sewage plan. And he couldn't work up any interest in that.

"There you are, you see," said Karli primly. "Another proof how little the young men of this town care for anything but their own pockets. They think nothing of the common good."

That riled me. It's easy to poke fun when you've got no real responsibilities. In our factory we are still paying out pensions to a whole heap of workers who had been a drag on the firm even in my grandfather's time. We all sit on top of each other in Nüssen, and there are not many jobs available. In the big cities you can fire whom you like: the Employment Bureau will step in and find other jobs for them. Nobody needs to feel guilty. My grandfather had no other choice, since he was on first-name terms with most of his workers. My uncle is more formal. I myself am familiar within limits and am for the unions but not for any one particular political party. If that won't work, I don't know what the hell would.

"Georg is a nice fellow," Karli said, "besides being rich, young, and good-natured. The Christian Union put him up because he knows a lot of farmers. The Free Voters will find him hard to beat. Both Sinz and Posselt realize that, and that's why they didn't beat each other up, but sat in the car wondering how best to hush the whole thing up. Posselt even offered to marry Frau Sinz after the divorce—when nothing at all had happened! That's what he gets for being too mean to go to Munich twice a month."

Heiner of course laughed, but I had not yet got it all clear in my mind. "Why didn't they beat each other up?"

"Because in Nüssen people of their sort don't do such things. It's the reputation that counts, not the woman."

"And Posselt has lost his," I said.

"No, Frau Sinz has," Karli said. "It's not unusual for a man to make a pass at a woman. The fact that nothing came of it doesn't hide the fact that something might have come of it. The trouble is that Frau Sinz is married, and people think there's bound to be something fishy going on if a man makes a pass at a married woman. Sinz is made to look like a fool in any case, since it was his wife. She didn't start it herself, that I can swear to, but people might still think she had started it."

"And now," said Heiner, "you're saying they thought first of their reputations and the coming elections?"

"What else could they think of?" Karli asked.

"Of Frau Sinz."

"Your interpretation stinks," said Heiner, and his ears began to redden. "But it's about what I'd expect. You're far too shallow to think of anything else."

"I can only think what everybody else thinks," said Karli.

"Let's go," I said. But Heiner and Karli were staring hard at each other and made no move. I went over to the counter and paid the bill. When I came back Heiner was just winding up. "It's quite natural that they didn't beat each other up, but it would have been equally natural if they had beaten each other up, whether Frau Sinz is good-looking or not. Posselt and Sinz were frightened of making themselves look ridiculous. They just didn't know what to do."

"But that's exactly what I've been saying," Karli cried, and at last he got to his feet. "The main thing was that nothing should be done. But don't say you pity either of them for not being man enough to get angry about it. What for, for God's sake? If

Posselt had made a proper job of it, nothing would have come out. For if Frau Sinz had had anything up top and if Posselt had grabbed properly and made enough of it to save himself a slap in the face, we should never have been told about it. Then everyone would be happy—either because they had got what they wanted or because they knew nothing about it. The real fault was Frau Sinz's."

Now Heiner stood up too, and we went off slowly.

"That's what I mean," Heiner said. "There are no true women any more, no true men and no true anger."

We drove off, each in his own car.

It was a useless time of day, not yet eight o'clock. What can you do on Saturdays at that time? It's too early even for the movies. And then I can easily start feeling guilty about my mother, sitting there at home with Grandmother and longing for a bit of young company. We went to Heiner's place and put on some records. He has a fantastic collection of over three hundred long-playing records. It's worth a small fortune.

Sitting with friends, listening to music, and drinking a bit induce a rare mood of well-being. You rock on your chair, take a sip from your glass, beat time, and the music makes you feel pleasantly easy with yourself. You think up clever answers which you would like to have made to someone or other but didn't think of in time. Then you feel annoyed with yourself, but take comfort in the thought that on the next occasion maybe you'll have them ready. Mäusle, the younger one of Heiner's sisters, came to join us. She still has her puppy fat.

"What are you sitting around here for?" she asked. "There's a dance on at the Hotel Schwan. The Antonio Trio from Kempten is playing."

Heiner wanted to send her back into the sitting room.

"Let her stay," I said. "The TV program is a bore on Saturdays."

"Mother never has it on anyway."

"How do you know there's a dance on?"

"I just know."

Karli and I were in favor of taking Mäusle along to the dance, but Heiner was unwilling, so we mucked around a bit more and flirted with Mäusle. In spite of all the clutter in Heiner's room I did a turn with her that sent the Persian rugs flying under the table.

Heiner began to get fidgety. I suppose he was ashamed that his sister was a girl. Sisters must never be girls, any more than mothers can be women. When Mäusle's skirt swung out and Karli commented admiringly on her legs Heiner did in fact laugh, but all the same he was embarrassed.

In the end we went off without Mäusle. Her mother, whom she fetched, also objected to her going along with us. Her elder sister was in bed with a sore throat, and Mäusle was on hospital duty. She was told to make some tea and find a play on the radio.

"I've had enough of this," Heiner said. "Why don't we go to Dachsler's or to Karli's place?"

Neither of us thought much of that idea. We were always at home. It was no place to work up a sense of occasion. I remember as a child finding that food in other people's houses tasted much better than in my own.

Nüssen has thirty-one taverns and four small breweries, because the town had been a junction for the wagon trade before the rail terminus was built with branch lines to Leutkirch and Kempten. Back in the Middle Ages the linen wagons from Augsburg had passed through Nüssen on their way to Italy—hence all the taverns for the drivers. The Hotel Schwan is of more recent vintage. My grandfather in his young days used to be a regular Sunday morning customer, and when I was still a kid we used to have a meal there once a month to give my mother a holiday from cooking.

Nowadays only salesmen and occasional tourists with partial board put up at the Schwan, which is falling apart wherever you look. What it needs is a new coat of paint and the hanging sign replaced by neon letters over the door. The cuisine is terrible too: none of us ever eats there. But they do have a big hall with a stage in which our local folklore society holds its annual Christmas binge. And occasionally the theater from Tübingen comes around with an operetta or a classical drama. The stage could be used much more than it is, if there were any real public for it. Once the local arts club tried putting on piano recitals and recitations. It kept going for three winters, and then the town had to make up the deficit. If you want to see a play or hear music you have to go to Munich or Zurich. With a three-hour drive you can be back home the same night.

A heap of cars was parked in front of the hotel, and even more motorcycles. The street was absolutely jammed. A policeman was directing the traffic, blowing his whistle and bawling at the farmer boys as they went buzzing around the hotel on their little machines, changing gear and stepping on the gas every time they passed him.

The hall was packed. The Antonio Trio—accordion, double bass, and percussion with lots of brass on the drums—sat on the stage in front of a painted backcloth of hills and vineyards. In the middle of the floor a space had been cleared for dancing, and the tables were pushed back against the walls. We could hardly get through to the bar.

"See anyone we know?" Karli asked.

They were all strangers to me except for a few girls from our factory. The air was so thick you could cut it with a knife. The band struck up again, and in the middle of the floor things began to simmer. But we reached the bar at last and got ourselves beer and a double slivovitz apiece.

"I don't think there's anything here for us," Heiner screamed in my ear. "I don't know a soul."

"What does it matter?"

"Tomorrow I'll have the whole shop full of stupid giggling girls."

There was nowhere for us to sit. All the tables were stacked with glasses and surrounded by young louts wearing suits which we had seen hanging for a year in the windows of the two haberdashers in the town. They sat there drinking, stamping, bawling, and laughing, outnumbering the girls two to one.

"This is God-awful," Karli screamed.

"Come on, let's get started," I screamed back.

"But where?" Heiner screamed.

"The plump one over there. She serves in the Café Motz. She's waiting for you."

Heiner turned her down with a grunt and reached for his slivovitz.

"Take a look at that one—where did she come from?"

Karli pointed to a slim blonde who was dancing with an arm right around the neck of a fellow we recognized—he had recently come to be physical training instructor at the Home for the Disabled, where the limbless are taught jobs.

"Not bad," Karli said. "Nice and tall."

"The fellow's an ass," Heiner said.

"What do you bet I'll get a dance?" I asked.

But Heiner was right. We didn't belong in the Schwan. Take my uncle's maid, for instance—a little dark mouse with tiny ears. I like her well enough, but why should I dance with her? All the same, I greeted her when she came past the counter in the arms of a fellow who also works for us and made her a sign that I wanted the next round with her. She nodded and said something to her partner, who squinted across at me. I knew the maid, a nice girl called Xeni, and all the others I had probably seen often enough in the street. Maybe even more of them worked for us than I recognized, or if not with us then in the textile factory or the paper warehouse. A lot of them were from the country: you can always tell those by their large hands and clumsy hairdos—not of course by their clothes, because nowadays they all dress alike. However, I thought to myself, if I dance with the housemaid nothing can go wrong. She's not unattractive and, though practically everybody knows who I am, they also know she works in my uncle's house. So it will all just look friendly and democratic.

The band started up again. I went quickly onto the floor and took her over from her glowering partner. "Thank you," I said. "My turn now. There are not many pretty girls here."

The boy went off without a murmur. I tucked Xeni under my right arm and we jogged off. There was hardly room to move. On all sides we were surrounded by damp hands, steaming backs, fat rumps, and panting mugs. They were singing, crashing into us, and some big yokel kicked me on the shin, but I swung up behind him with Xeni and, with a backward turn, got one home that put him right off his stroke. By the time he had turned to see who it was we had slid off into the crowd.

"Not so fast," Xeni said, laughing. "We're not breaking records."

"Don't you like it?"

"I do, of course."

I steered her around toward the bar. Heiner and Karli were standing there with their heads close together. They laughed and pointed in our direction, and Karli held up his glass.

Xeni really is a cute little thing, and quick on the uptake too. She responded to the slighest pressure, was with me in all the turns, and danced all the more complicated steps that came into my mind. In a roughhouse like this you have to hop up and down across the rhythm, just hint at it, utilize pauses for turns, holding the body straight and guiding with only a slight movement of the hips. These yokels with their waggling bottoms have no idea: dripping with sweat, they jog around with their girls like slabs of jelly, hacking their way through the other couples like lumberjacks clearing the undergrowth.

"Enjoying it?"

"Oh yes."

She was just dancing, not chatting as she does at my aunt's, reeling off recipes by the hour. The flesh was firm on her back. I put my thumb under the strap of her brassière or pressed into her shoulder blade with the side of my hand. Then after a couple of more beats I felt her stomach. Now and again we exchanged quick glances. She had a sort of heat haze around the eyes. It was all very delicious. When the number came to an end we moved across to the bar.

"Congratulations," Heiner said. "A champion pair."

"What may we offer the lady?" Karli asked.

I suggested various things, and in the end she allowed me to buy her a coke. Karli wanted to pour a framboise into it, but she wouldn't let him. Very soon I noticed she was squinting across at the table where the boy was sitting with whom she had been dancing previously. Before I could get a word in, Karli bowed and asked for the next dance. And after that Heiner did exactly the same.

A troop of motorcyclists came up swinging their crash helmets in their hands, and crowded me off the bar. I just had time to snatch my beer and then found myself standing like a fool wedged between two tables. Some girls giggled behind me and somebody spoke my name. Karli had vanished. Heiner was still dancing. I felt I had had enough.

At the door I met Karli again. The two Gürtler brothers were with him—Achim and Wolf, large blond giants with chiseled torsos. They had already been drinking and their fluffy cheeks were aflame. But they stood firm when some lout crashed into them, riding on top of the rabble pushing its way in and out of the hall with sovereign disdain. Wolf is a house surgeon at the local hospital, where his father, now a G.P. in the town, had also begun. Achim qualified as a vet a year ago and is now in Friedrichshafen doing his first job as a substitute. He spends most weekends back home in Nüssen. We call them Brother Man and Brother Beast.

"The town seems busy tonight," Achim said.

"There was semolina for supper at the hospital," said Wolf, "so I broke out."

"Where have you just come from?" I asked.

They had been in the Traube. The Tennis Club was having a get-together in the back room—not a scheduled one, but with the hazy intention of making a night of it.

"You come along too," said Brother Beast. "They're all falling asleep. We'll get things moving."

"Who's there?" Karli asked.

"The whole bunch," Brother Man grumbled. "All the people I should love to have on the operating table. Only our old dad is lacking. We must seize our chance."

We spread out in search of Heiner. He had stopped dancing and was standing in a corner with no light for his cigarette.

"Where did you get to?" he asked.

"Are you coming to the Tennis Club with us?"

"Who's there?"

After the sizzling atmosphere of the Schwan the back room of the Traube felt like a tomb. Tiled stove, paneled walls, polished parquet flooring, pewter mugs on the plate rail, and all the well-known faces sitting upright at tables in family groups as they always sit, with Posselt at the head. Rapsmeier, our champion tennis player and reputedly the best-looking man in Nüssen, was busy totting up a list, a green money box on the table in front of him. He gave us a savage nod. In the whole of five years, ever since he's been working at the bank, he has not been able to get rid of his damned honorary job. If there were evening classes in Nüssen, ten to one he'd have a hand in them too.

Karli and I ventured in first, the brothers trundling along behind us. We sang out a moderately loud "good evening" and made a slight bow, at the same time scanning the tables at lightning speed in a search for the best place to sit. Over on the left beside the stove, at a comfortable distance, sat the young set and—even more important—the Reutles.

We scuttled across the parquet flooring in their direction, sat down with a sigh of relief, and looked back for the others. Heiner made it with two silent bows toward the presidential table. The Gürtler brothers were nowhere in sight.

"So we meet again," said Phrosine. I didn't notice anything in her manner; she seemed to have thawed out again.

"I hear you were out at the chalet," Georg remarked. "It's a full week since I managed a swim. What a grind—every day somewhere else! I feel I've earned my evening drink."

The door flew open again, the talk died down, and the brothers came clattering in. They grinned at the family tables and called out, "Where have you got to? Oh, there you are."

Without a word of greeting they dragged each other by the arm across to us and came to rest on the corner seat.

"Damn slippery floor," said Brother Man.

"Should put sand on it," Brother Beast rasped.

"Waiter," Georg called quickly. He knew the brothers from nightly sessions in his house.

"They're putting their heads together," Karli hissed. "Watch out for trouble—the families are gathering."

"So what?" said Achim loudly. "Waiter!"

They got their beer and tipped it down. So things were all right for the moment. The family tables relaxed their sickly smiles.

It was important to keep on drinking, otherwise we would go under. Georg stood a round of champagne to go with the beer. The brothers refused it, but Heiner, Karli, and I accepted gratefully. It's a combination with a very lively kick.

Phrosine was wearing a new dress. We complimented her on it. It was pale blue, and with her bare brown shoulders and short wavy hair above she looked good—like something out of the book of old Italian Masters I've got at home.

The party spirit was beginning to flag, and we all got quieter and quieter. The brothers were each as drunk as the other. They sat blinking at the walls and hadn't a word to say for themselves either. Georg tried ordering more schnapps for them, but not even that raised a flicker. They can go on for hours in this state of silent contentment. There was nothing for us at the next table either. The boys and girls there were too young— all of them around twenty, and they have their own particular atmosphere.

Suddenly Posselt got to his feet. "Let's dance," he said. "We don't often get a chance to be merry together."

The youngsters must have been tipped off in advance, for they produced an automatic record-player on the spot. Phrosine was snapped up at once, Heiner and Karli both getting up together. I didn't mind. I went over to the family tables to drink a glass of wine with Rapsmeier.

For the first dance all the married men took their wives, and mixing did not begin until the second. Sinz was the only one to stick religiously to his apothecary wife, while Posselt stayed firm in his chair. I became aware at last that he had his daughter with him.

As I've already said, Ruth plays the organ. She parts her hair in the middle and is not pretty—more like a ripe walnut with the green leaves still around it. Maybe in time she'll get fat. But I like the way she walks through the town with her music-case under her arm, greeting everyone with a precise nod. Sitting beside her dashing little father, she appeared to be keeping a careful watch over him. I asked Rapsmeier if he knew anything about her. After all, he works in the bank and so must get to know a lot about people, but it seems the idea has never even occurred to him. So I invited Ruth to dance.

I was soon sweating as I revolved and rattled around the floor with Ruth. Then her father had a go, sweeping her into all corners of the room in a passionate tango. After that he returned her to me. We let ourselves go in a slinky slow foxtrot which I savored deliciously, getting to know the girl better in the process. But in the middle of a long undulation, when I had just got my shoulder close to her bosom, Karli came up and asked me if I was going with them to the hospital. It seems that Brother Wolf, who was sitting upright in his corner, flames rising from his collar he was so drunk, was supposed to be on night duty. He was insisting that we should all go along with him, for he got bored on his own.

I took the suggestion as a joke, and we went on dancing. When the first batch of ten records came to an end there was an intermission. Ruth and I joined the others at the table.

Beside Wolf stood a case of beer all ready to be transported to the hospital. Phrosine wanted to go along, Heiner and Karli too of course. Georg shook his head, while Ruth looked embarrassed. She hasn't had much experience with people.

"We must go along to the hospital and give Wolf a hand," said Brother Vet. "We must do something."

"You're right," Karli said. "We've been all over the place, but never in the hospital. And after all we're medical men—we have the right."

I had swallowed down a couple of framboises too quickly and was ready to fall in with any suggestion.

Wolf pointed to the door. "You see him?" he cried. "An interesting case. We must find out whether his blood is different. That would prove it."

The young potter was standing at the door, without his friend, the watchmaker from Ratzenried. The nice boy was looking a bit disheveled in his green suit—not a bit like the usual weekend trip to the mountains. He was smiling nervously at us.

"He's in trouble," Karli said softly. "Either the motorbike's broken down or he's been transferred."

Phrosine laughed and wanted to know if what people said about him was really true.

"Klaus," Wolf called out, "come here."

"Klaus, come along, Klaus!" we all cried.

Klaus came, and was given something to drink. He was already a bit the worse for wear and so miserable that he tipped back everything we put into his hand.

"Klaus is wonderful," Wolf said.

Then the music began again, and Phrosine wanted to dance with Klaus. But Klaus, politely trying his best, could not get up from the table. We laughed a lot, Klaus included.

"I must go back on duty," Wolf urged. "They don't know I'm here. If anything happens I'll have to become a vet."

We all grabbed each other and struggled to our feet. The room fell suddenly silent. The family tables were staring, and some of the dancing couples were standing stock-still, among them Ruth and Brother Achim. I hadn't even noticed that they had gone off to dance.

"I propose," said Posselt, "that we push the tables together and mix."

Wolf beamed, nodded, and opened his mouth to say something, but Karli punched him in the side and whispered, "Shut your mouth, you fool, and get out."

Somehow or other we managed it. We withdrew in a solid cluster, with Klaus and the case of beer in the middle. Karli even found time to make our excuses. Very quickly he mumbled

that we had had a bit too much to drink and were rather noisy
—it was better that we should go. Posselt waved his hand understandingly and the family tables smiled and nodded. Ruth
was standing with Brother Vet beside the phonograph, sorting
out titles. I was still thinking of her a little.

Outside Wolf said, "We'll make a blood test. We must find
out."

We piled into Phrosine's car, all six of us with the case of beer,
and drove off.

"Where's Georg?"

"He's got his own car," Phrosine said.

"Hurry," said Wolf. "Night duty."

Phrosine drove around past the woods and switched off the
engine as we sped down the hill and in through the hospital
gates. We got out and crept quietly through the little door leading to the kitchens. Wolf led the way, the case of beer supported
on his hip as if it were a carton of dry milk. The hospital was still
as death. Emergency lights were burning in the corridors.
Phrosine skidded on the polished linoleum. We just managed
to catch her, made a seat of our hands, and bore her in a gallop
into the room where Wolf stood beckoning.

"In you come. Shut the door. Saved!"

The room was lined from top to bottom with white tiles.
Against one wall there stood an intricate metal bed, with an
oilcloth cover and levers beneath. There were glass cabinets
full of surgical instruments. Over a wooden rack hung with test
tubes water was running into a large basin from three rubber
tubes.

"Drink up now—don't be shy," said Wolf. He was getting into
a white smock. We wanted them too. Then each of us took a
bottle of beer and opened it. Wolf produced a plastic flask containing cognac from one of the cabinets.

"On with your aprons."

"Who's going to start?" said Phrosine.

Wordlessly we flitted about the room in our white gowns.
Each of us had something in his hand: Heiner was plucking
cotton wool with a pair of tweezers, Karli swinging a sort of

fish-knife, Phrosine was beating the water basin with a piece of rubber tubing, while I was fixing a piece of adhesive bandage on the wall.

"This isn't going to hurt," said Wolf, holding a syringe up to the light. "I'll show you first how it's done. There's another syringe lying ready on the table for the next one. Klaus, my little man, are you afraid?"

Klaus was even drunker than the rest of us. He stood there swaying from side to side and smiling. Obediently he took off his jacket, then his shirt, and was already fumbling at his trousers when we seized him and laid him down on the couch. Wolf covered him with a rubber apron.

"We're going to mix your blood with Phrosine's blood," he said.

"We'll make a completely new man of you," said Karli.

Swinging our instruments, we did a war dance around the couch, prodding our sacrificial lamb, but Klaus was not to be roused. He just nodded, flexed his arm, and smiled expectantly. Phrosine shivered.

"Klaus, my hero," Wolf whispered, "I am now going to make you happy." He took aim with the syringe, screwed up his eyes, lowered the needle and plunged it in, then, letting out his breath, pulled back the piston. We kept our eyes on the syringe, in which the bubbling juice was rising, while Klaus nodded, faster and faster, smiled and giggled.

Wolf withdrew the needle, handed the syringe to me, and took up the other from the table.

"Now, Phrosine."

She hesitated. We lifted her up and laid her down beside Klaus. And before she had time to resist the needle was in her arm.

"There we are, my sweet."

She turned pale and stared at the syringe. "Let's see which is darker," she said.

Aiming my syringe, I shot a thin stream of Klaus's blood onto the tiled wall. It made a pretty pattern. With a groan Karli snatched the second syringe from Wolf's hand and shot too.

"It's a boy!" he shouted. "Come on, Dachsler, spray a girl on it. We'll have a wedding."

I made another shot. Karli stooped down and took aim from below at my big blot, which had immediately begun to wilt and was running down the wall. Spray poured down over the swelling bag.

"What a lot of kids!"

Klaus and Phrosine sat bolt upright, side by side on the couch. We could hear ourselves breathing.

"Spurt it out," Wolf cried out behind me. "Spurt it all over."

At that moment a telephone rang. Startled, I pressed the piston of my syringe, and a spot of blood hit Karli on the cheek. Wolf ran to the corner and picked up the phone. We stood still. There had been an accident. Someone had fallen off his motorcycle. He would be arriving directly: the ambulance was on its way.

In silence we got to work clearing up. Phrosine helped Klaus to dress, Heiner wiped the wall clean with a rag, Wolf dismantled the syringes under the tap, Karli and I put beer bottles back into the case and carried it out into the corridor.

"Get out through the basement," Wolf said.

We hurried off down the stairs. From a side corridor we heard the clump of flat heels approaching.

"The night sister," Wolf whispered. He ran back up the stairs and into the side corridor. We pressed ourselves against the wall as he spoke to the sister and then went off with her. In a tight bunch we squeezed through the narrow door and closed it behind us.

We were in the car before we noticed that Klaus was missing. I got out and went back. The door had a safety lock and could not be opened from the outside. Somebody was tapping on the glass window in its upper half.

"Is that you, Klaus?"

"Open up," I heard him wail indistinctly.

I spoke to him through the keyhole, telling him to try the door from the inside. Klaus scratched about, then the little window flew open and I saw Klaus's head framed in it. He stood there smiling at me, gentler and even drunker than before. There was nothing for it but to drag him out through the window opening. Klaus hoisted himself up willingly enough and poked his head through, but then got himself wedged in an awkward position with an arm jammed under his chest and couldn't ease himself forward. He groaned and gurgled, his face getting darker and darker. I seized him by the shoulders, hung on him, put my feet up against the door so that I was suspended at an angle in the air beneath him. His pelvis was stuck fast. With a rocking movement we got it free and he fell to the ground in a heap in the glare of the headlights. Quickly we scrambled into the car and away before the ambulance arrived.

Phrosine sped off up the hill into the town. We were laughing our heads off and drinking foaming beer from the bottle in spite of the lurching and jogging of the car.

"Incredible," Heiner cried. "Have you ever known anything like it?"

"And now Wolf has an accident on his hands."

"Let's hope he doesn't get things confused."

We noticed that Phrosine had driven right through the town and was now turning off across the fields.

"Where are you going?"

"Swimming," she cried.

That was a wonderful idea. We started to undress immediately. It was a bit of a scrimmage, since all of us were in the back of the car—I on Karli's knee and Klaus lying on top of us all. He was happy of course, for it was warm and wherever he felt he encountered male flesh and bones. He peeled off his shirt and giggled when we tore at his trousers. The car lurched along the dried-up riverbed, skidding and throwing up stones as we headed for the deep pit the river Wertach had scooped out of the soft subsoil. We sat in the back in our underpants.

The pool is full even in summer when the flow of water down the valley may be no more than a hand's-breadth. Phrosine stopped. "Everyone out and swim."

We clambered out of the car and hopped over the stones. In

the glare of the headlights the water in the pool looked black. Heiner threw in a chip of rock. My teeth were chattering, for the air was quite cold.

"Yellowbelly," I heard Karli say.

Heiner cast a guilty glance down his front. "Damn it," he shouted, "where's Klaus?"

Klaus was still in the car, where he had fallen into a doze. We dragged him out and, holding him by the arms and legs, waded out along the rocky bottom up to our knees. At that point there is a sheer downward drop. Heiner almost toppled over, Karli slithered, and I stumbled too, for the water was cold and had numbed me. Anyway, Klaus fell in. Behind us Phrosine sounded the horn.

Klaus surfaced at once, gasped, and rotated away again.

"After him," I shouted, jumped right in, and got my hand on a piece of his underpants. It was lucky there were three of us, for the boy was already lashing around. Treading water, we pushed him up against the rocky ledge. The headlights were shining in our faces and we could hardly see a thing. And all the time Phrosine kept sounding the horn like a lunatic.

We dragged Klaus from the water and stood him on his feet. He was coughing and shivering and his skin felt clammy. But he was all right.

I was busy banging him on the back when suddenly Heiner and Karli let out a shout and shot off across the gravel. Then we were enveloped in darkness. Still sounding the horn, Phrosine was backing the car away down the riverbed. It turned, the headlights swept over us once more, and then the car vanished into the woods. Between the trees we saw the beam of light getting smaller and smaller.

"What a filthy trick!"

"What about our clothes?"

"We've got nothing to dry ourselves with."

We felt around every inch of the ground, stubbing and bruising our toes, but our clothes were still with Phrosine in the car.

"Come on, we'll have to walk," Karli said.

"But we've only got pants on."

"Can't be helped," I said. "Take them off and give them a wring. They'll do to dry ourselves a bit."

But it didn't help much. The cold was already rattling my bones. We had to get back home as soon as possible or we should all have pneumonia tomorrow.

"That swine Phrosine," Heiner chattered. "Wait till I get hold of her."

It was no longer funny. We limped along the riverbed and up to the road. It was sandy there, and the going was better. Karli set a brisk trotting pace, to get us warmed up. Oddly enough, Klaus had not a word to say, but kept bravely up with us. He had almost more wind than we.

I felt mad with rage, having to run home like that in the middle of the night, practically naked, wet and freezing—and God knows whom we might meet on the way. Klaus's brief underpants bobbed up and down in front of me. I tried to overtake him, but he had no difficulty in keeping ahead. It wasn't his fault of course, but you can't stop all sorts of silly ideas from coming into your head when you're in a rage and have no one to vent it on, let alone having to run a cross-country race for the sake of your health. Karli, Heiner, and I—we ought to spread him across the next milestone, I thought, and do him— all three on top of him or however it is they manage it. Our pace had slackened and we were panting.

Klaus saw the pile first: our shirts, shoes, socks, trousers, and jackets lying in a heap in the middle of the road. Never have I got dressed so quickly, though everything was gritty and scratched my skin. None of us had had the sense to take off our wet underpants first. The feel of them gradually drying as we walked along was very unpleasant.

We marched on in silence, and in half an hour we had reached the edge of the town. Klaus was the first to take his leave. He shook us all by the hand and thanked us for a pleasant evening. That could have been funny, but we were all too tired to respond. The three of us walked on and then one after another dropped out, each to his own home.

On Sunday morning I had a headache. I took my mother and my grandmother out to lunch at Miggersreuth, where a new hotel had just been opened. The food was excellent. My grandmother had her favorite dish—veal fricassee with noodles in bread crumbs. My mother and I had a steak. The meat was just right and the peas were so fresh they tasted of milk. The view was fantastic. The hotel stands on a rise, with an unobstructed view. There was a mild breeze, and the air was so clear that we could see everything from the Oberstdorfer mountains to the Three Sisters in the Swiss range. After the meal my headache was gone.

For the Little Ones
and the Big Ones

He had stage fright again. He wiped his damp hands on his trousers as the children whispered behind his back. He gave them a warning look before turning away to peep through the curtain. The lights were on, the cameras ranged in a semicircle around the little stage, and the music was beginning to fade. They would be on directly. And of course he had forgotten his words. He screwed up his face and murmured into the microphone which hung from his neck over the front of his thick woolen shirt. The shirt made him fat around the hips, but otherwise he looked young and dashing. His hair hanging down over his forehead made him one of them—a young comrade. "Hello there, girls and boys," he said, and then tried again a bit higher. "Hello there, boys and girls." Anyway he would mention the boys first.

"Quiet," came the gruff voice from the top of the studio. "We begin in twenty seconds from now. Rudolf, keep still and don't let the microphone bump on your chest."

"I never let anything bump," Pössner replied.

Old Gramel was up there at the director's desk, sitting in the comfortable swivel chair with sweatholes in the back. He would probably be fondling his fat belly, his tenderly nurtured paunch, lying loose and relaxed inside his light trousers. Beside him the little blonde girl would be hovering over her buttons on the control desk and watching the three little screens in front of her. She was anxious to do things right for Gramel, and it wasn't really her fault that there wasn't enough in her head to make even an air hostess of her. The sound engineer would be muttering and fiddling with his knobs behind them. Louder, softer—always glad of an excuse to chatter. In the adjoining room behind the glass panel the music engineer was threading tapes on the machines.

A gong boomed, and then the continuity girl was announcing them. "And now, for our young viewers, here is Rudolf Pössner again with his program 'Think It Over.' Enjoy yourselves."

The opening music began—a nice crisp tune which kept going through the title shots. Pössner creased up the corners of his eyes and passed with a flourish through the curtain. "Hello there, boys and girls. Today we're going to give you three more big nuts to crack. Think them over and then write down your answers on a postcard. We shall put all the correct ones in a hat, then pick out ten of them, and the lucky ten—yes, the lucky ten—" In front of him the little black hole of the camera lens waited, to the left of it stood an assistant floor manager, yawning. Grin, he told himself, and looked even straighter into the eyes of the million and a half tots who were now sitting in front of their television screens, and whose mothers and grandmothers were glad to have them sitting there, for at five o'clock on a Sunday afternoon they are worn out.

"As I was saying," he said, and laughed, "the lucky ten will be asked to come to the studio and take part in the next program. So now's your chance. Pay attention and think hard. You know what's coming now." And with that Pössner leaped elastically in his tight trousers on the boards, grabbed a corner of the curtain, and, still facing the camera with the red light, said, "The children from the Bollhardt School in Karlsruhe are all ready to start. So here's our first picture puzzle."

He pulled back the curtain, and that was it. During the next ten minutes the eight schoolchildren would be doing their charade based on the nursery rhyme about the fox stealing the goose. The farmer, whiskers stuck on his upper lip and a spade in his hand, swept onto the stage, bawling at the goose girl, who held tight to her overlong skirt. They were much too loud. The sound engineer seated on his two-wheeler hastily wound back the microphone gantry and nodded vigorously.

Pössner crept away through the studio. The skin on his face felt tight under the grease paint. People with nothing to do were standing in front of a studio screen, watching the pictures which were now going out over the transmitting masts. "Where are the prize lambs?" he whispered in the floor manager's ear. "I want them now." Under the floor manager's guidance they filed out of the dressing room, the ten winners of last week's competition. They lined up on a platform in the studio, standing stiffly in their starched clothes and white socks, the boys with bow ties and partings straight as arrows. Among them was a girl of fourteen or so with lipstick on and a shiny handbag dangling from her arm. Gramel's secretary had slipped again. The draw always had to be rigged a little bit. The children came by plane or sleeper from far places, and had to be shipped off home again in the evening.

The pace of the charade got faster and faster. The goose was already gone. The farmer was making a speech to the local council, squinting through his glasses. The maid came in crying and tripping over her feet. The goose, the goose! The farmer and the mayor ran off, sending the benches flying. On the next set the farm boy was standing in front of the farmhouse, picking his nose. But he didn't fall into the water trough. They'd rehearsed it well.

Pössner was now standing beside Fräulein Kaus, who had a recorder in her hand and was giving the note for a song. There were little pearls of sweat on her upper lip. She was a teacher at the Karlsruhe school, and the charades were her idea. She had come to Gramel one day and said she wanted to do something with her children. They weren't from the best parts of the town, but they were bright, and the school was a bit run-down. So, from her slight knowledge of psychology, the prospects were promising. Gramel, with his sensitive nose for sharing the load, had realized at once that this earnest little woman could give him something worth putting out.

Pössner smiled at her. She smiled back. Still blowing, she crept out of camera range toward the stage, emphasizing the beat, since her pupils were dragging. She even played more softly as she got closer to the microphone. She thought of everything.

There were the cameras, and behind them the cameramen—all slim youngsters who were supposed to be learning their jobs on children's programs, though it is not always easy, since amateurs of course never stick to their drilled movements and positions like experienced actors, but in performance speed everything up. Behind the camermen stood the assistant floor managers—boys in tennis shoes and maybe one or two onion-shaped girls from the neighboring art school. Their job was to watch the cable behind the moving camera and keep it out of the way. Very boring work. Behind them all was the chief cameraman, lying back in his little soft seat and watching the pictures. He didn't operate a camera: his job was to arrange the lights beforehand—that's to say, not he personally, but now and again he put in a word to the effect that something should be brighter or not so bright. The technical operations manager then pressed buttons to raise or lower the lamps or told the electricians to open or close the shutters on this or that lamp. At the very back, wedged in between steel scaffolding, sat the continuity announcer. She had to speak a few sentences before and after each program and maybe appear again in the evening. The girl doing the children's program was a new one on probation. She had once dreamed of becoming an actress, and now of course the chance was gone. All she had to do was to put on her make-up, set her hair, smile, say her little piece, wait around a couple of hours, smile again, and do her closing announcement. There was no one else in the studio. Those who had nothing to do moved around quietly, and outside the door the red light pulsed, warning people not to come in.

Pössner was due on again. He took up his position on a chalk cross on the cement floor beside the stage, turned his head away from the camera, and then, as the schoolchildren spoke their last sentence, swung his eyes around toward the camera on his left to make it look spontaneous, and said:

"There, now you've seen the first picture puzzle, and we hope you found it amusing. You've probably got the answer. It wasn't very difficult, was it? Now this is what we want to know: What is the title of the song the girls and boys from

Karlsruhe have just been acting? If any of you don't know—
and I don't think that can be many of you—I suggest you ask
your granny. She'll know for sure. And if you haven't got a
granny—" He was stuck again. The millions of infants sitting
in front of their screens floated past his eyes—he would like to
wallop their bottoms and send them out to play. Giving himself
an angry jab, he found the thread again and went on, "Well, in
that case you won't find the answer, and I'm very sorry for
you. And now let's meet the winners of last week's program."

The picture on the screen slid off Pössner toward the children
on the platform, who stared obediently at the camera with
the red light. He went across to them and pushed his way into
the middle. Smiling, youthful, he spoke his piece.

"Well, here they are, the clever ten who are our guests in the
studio today. What's your name? And yours? Did you come by
plane? Were you sick? What, you drank some coffee? That was
brave of you. So here we have Mathilde from Berlin, Gert
from Hanover, Rudi from Munich, little Lola from Böblingen,
Joachim, Kurt, and—what was your name? Bibi?"

"Yes, I'm called Bibi," said a little boy in green, "but not in
school. That's my name at home." He climbed down from the
platform and ran to Pössner. Pössner turned him toward the
camera and let him talk. This was a real gift from the gods:
you didn't get something so fresh and lively in a program every
day, and certainly never from grownups.

"I've brought something for you," Bibi said. "A present from
my mummy with her love."

He handed Pössner a box which contained a portrait of Bibi.
Pössner held it up to the camera, so that Gramel could get it
in close-up.

"I've signed the picture myself," Bibi said, "and I can write
my whole address myself too. Will we have the Punch and Judy
now?"

"Yes, we'll have Punch and Judy directly."

"Then I like you very much," Bibi said and toddled back to
his seat.

Pössner led the children in the usual way past the cameras

to the puppet booth and sat them down on the benches in front of it.

"They'll be here in a moment," he said. "What would you like to see today?"

The youngest ones suggested Billy in the Clock Case or Snow White, Red Riding Hood, cops and robbers, or nothing at all. Pössner sat down beside the fourteen-year-old girl, who was sitting with a straight face on the very edge of the third bench. "And what about you?" he asked. "Can I use your Christian name, or ought I to call you Miss?" She lowered her head. Now he would show the millions of moms and uncles sitting in their kitchens or living rooms beside the children what he could do. It might even induce the radio magazines to print his name in full at last.

"I like Punch and Judy, don't you?" he said. "We're not all that grown-up yet. Or do you prefer the movies?"

She lowered her head still further, not answering, and Pössner saw that her neck was growing red. Before he could put any further questions, Bibi popped up to observe that his daddy made his own movies at home. They had films of Mummy picking flowers, of mountains, and Mummy in a boat on the lake. Bibi was sometimes in them too, very tiny and in color. He had often watched himself.

A camera came pushing in from the left, to catch Bibi in close-up. Pössner saw it coming and pulled the little boy over to him. Would he like to tell the shy auntie all about Punch and Judy?

"Kill her!" Bibi cried. "Let Punch kill them all—pull off Auntie's head like with my crocodile. Punch gets an ax, but Auntie doesn't."

The man who worked the puppets came out quickly from his booth. In his dignified way he told the children that Punch was waiting eagerly to entertain his guests, but first he wanted to know whether the children had a long way to go to school, and whether it was dangerous. All of them said yes, except for Bibi, who went to his kindergarten by car. Splendid, said the puppet-master, and of course they were all good children, weren't they?

Pössner felt like giving Bibi a pinch, but the show must go on. He slipped off the bench out of camera range and looked up at the glass control room, where Gramel sat watching the pictures on his three screens. He had an arm around the vision mixer and was pressing her shoulder each time he spoke the number of the screen he wanted to use.

"Happy?" he whispered in the teacher's ear.

"Yes," she breathed back, and Pössner pushed his cheek near to hers. He would be on again shortly. He moved across to the trampoline which had been erected in the middle of the studio. Markus Hügi was not yet in the studio—he was probably getting his make-up checked. Years ago Hügi had run a youth hostel, but he gave it up to join a circus. From the top of a floating crane in Kiel harbor he had dived a hundred and fifty feet into the water and so got himself on the newsreels. After that he had been able to earn his living as a stunt man. He had cycled across roofs, jumped into tarpaulins, leaped from moving cars, and been dragged on his stomach through lakes of burning oil. He had doubled in films, been trampled by horses, fallen dead over cliffs, and been thrown head-first through cardboard walls. Now and again he appeared in commercials, displaying a bandaged arm and observing with a smile that he could afford to do such things on the excellent insurance policy he had. Hügi had earned a lot of money, and he drove around in red cars. But as he got older he began to worry about whether he would always have enough money. He started up a laundry, which didn't go properly, and he even tried his hand at a luxury bar fitted in wood and brass. But Hügi doesn't smoke and gets suddenly sleepy every night at the stroke of ten. And so for some years now he had been doing children's programs on TV, and would go on as long as the young people still remembered him as a daredevil stunt man and he could get a reasonable fee.

Hügi came in and tested the trampoline. Then he moved a few steps to the side and waited for his cue. The children were clapping. The Punch and Judy was over, and Pössner was back on the screen.

"Now we have a new surprise," he said, "tied up with our second puzzle. A man you all know will tell you what you have to do. It is—yes—!"

He flung out his hand and laughed genially in the direction of Hügi, who tripped forward on springy feet and said, "Thank you very much. I'm delighted to be here."

"We're delighted too," said Pössner.

"I think you've got a very fine program," said Hügi.

"Nice of you to say so," said Pössner.

"I would go so far as to say it's the finest program I've ever been invited to appear in," said Hügi.

"I had no idea," said Pössner.

"We athletes and artistes need an audience to inspire us," said Hügi.

"I'm dying to know what you'll be doing for us today," said Pössner.

"When I was working in the circus," said Hügi, "and what a grand time it was, the following thing once happened to me—"

Pössner left Hügi talking and walked away. Angrily he flung himself down beside the children on the cement floor and did ten quick push-ups. The children were staring in fascination as Hügi continued to tell them about his life in the circus. After that he would tell the story about the tiny pair of swim-trunks his dear old mother from Munich had sewn for him as a mascot, and how once at a swimming contest et cetera. Anyway, Hügi was on, and would do a few turns on the trampoline, and then there would be a short film in which a disguised Hügi would do something mad, which would be either right or wrong—that was the problem the children had to solve. Finally he would speak a few sentences on body-building and sports and then make the point that if he had paid more attention in school he could have become something else—but what? All of that would take ten minutes. Pössner wandered off to the make-up room.

The make-up girl, who came from Yugoslavia and was learning the job, was not there. She would probably be in the big studio, where the ballet had been rehearsing bits of a musical for days now. Of course there would be masses of eyebrow work and large areas of flesh for her to slap grease paint on.

Pössner sat down in the barber's chair and regarded himself in the mirror. Pössner is thirty years old exactly. He has an efficiency apartment with a kitchenette and toilet of his own, and he has a motor scooter too. His nose is decorative, without much character, but it makes him look young. He is a bit full in the face perhaps, but on that account is free from wrinkles. With a light tan make-up he doesn't look bad; the large strong buddy, the pleasant-mannered young man with a nice laugh and a twinkle at the back of his eye. He has hairs on his chest and legs and is quite good at English and French. He is quick on the uptake and at ease in company. He has reason to be pleased with himself: if not an actor, he is at least a programs man, who does his own afternoon show and appears before the cameras. Eventually he will be given a chance to direct and will work his way up to evening programs. He spent two years on a newspaper before going into television. The newspaper work had been quite unnecessary, as he realized later. Pössner knows nothing about electronics: that's what the men and women in white overalls are there for, he says.

When you dry up in front of the camera, Pössner thought to himself, you mustn't whatever you do start wondering how many people are watching you. This afternoon my image is flickering in perhaps three million households—that's about seven million people. I could shock the whole lot rigid at one go. Quick as lightning shirt up, pants down, and show them my bare bottom. I ought to terrify them, make them howl. There wouldn't be much time—Gramel would flap and then black me out. Or better still, I could put on my most sincere expression and say chummily, Ladies, now I am speaking to you. You must sleep with more men. Pass it on.

The floor manager fetched him from the make-up room. He went back to the children. In the middle of the studio Markus Hügi was still talking about himself and giving his young audience sporting hints. Then a camera took Pössner up.

"Come on, kids, all of you—to the world's biggest construction kit. Today we're going to build ourselves a bulldozer."

They moved across to another corner of the studio, where there was a large platform piled up with bits and pieces. The children sat down on the floor in front of it, and Pössner set to work.

It had been his idea to construct machines during the program—not models, but almost life-size machines or even, in some cases, blown-up ones, so you could see what was going on. The wooden parts were prefabricated in the carpenter's shop and designed to fit together as easily as possible, so that Pössner could assemble the whole machine within fifteen minutes. The separate parts had to be of simple design, the blocks and planes identifiable at a glance, and above all the machine must work. Pössner would start practicing days ahead on fitting the parts together. He oiled screws, soaped pegs, had the bits that stuck planed, and was always shouting for the carpenter since nothing ever went smoothly. He needed to be able to assemble the machine smoothly while describing it and its parts. He had already built a locomotive that steamed, a roller that could be set in motion by a manually operated crank, a double-decker bus and an oversize combustion engine with moving pistons.

The base and caterpillar treads of the bulldozer were already screwed firm to the platform. Pössner stuck in the driver's cabin and fixed up the cable drum. The effort made him groan, and he got a strong boy to help him raise the crane jib. In trying to fix the jib he dropped the nut from his trembling fingers.

"My daddy can do that better," Bibi called out.

"Pity he isn't here."

"My daddy's got a workshop in the cellar, and he makes things when he's feeling low."

"That's always the best way," said Pössner, getting the screw home at last. He turned away in relief and stared at Bibi in restrained fury. "I wish your daddy a lot more Bibis."

He inserted the grab and pulled the cable firm. Then he got up on the driver's seat and tapped twice with his foot against the side. This was the signal for the stagehand lying on the floor behind the bulldozer to turn the platform from side to side and revolve the treads. Simultaneously the sound engineer mixed in the noise of motors and rattling chains.

It must have made a good picture, with the bulldozer moving back and forth and the grab being raised and lowered and opened and shut at the same time.

Pössner spun the cable drum around with both hands, being careful to note which cable was for the grab and which for the crane jib. It was quite strenuous work. Suddenly a metal clip shot from the boards beneath his feet. The grab fell with a crash and the cable drum frame whipped up sharply past his head to clatter down at the front of the platform. The children sprang to their feet. Pössner's forehead was hurting. Blood streamed down and a big drop spread out over his woolen shirt. He gathered his wits quickly and said into the camera lens:

"Nothing's happened. Don't be frightened. I'm still alive." He licked the blood from a finger and smiled—the brave soldier. "Dear mothers at home in front of the television screen, your children are safe and unharmed. Only Bibi—now what's the matter with Bibi?"

Bibi was crying, his face all tears and misery. Pössner got down from the platform and took Bibi up in his arms. Now was the moment. Ladies, I am speaking to you— But instead he said it was time for the third problem, which was a very funny one. At once the drama students waiting on another set began to declaim. It was a touching picture: Pössner with streams of blood on his face and a tiny weeping boy cuddled under his chin.

The students were doing a dramatic version of the proverb, "The cobbler should stick to his last." A tenor comes to the cobbler to collect his shoes, but he has no money to pay for them. The cobbler admires the tenor's voice, they decide to change jobs—with ensuing complications until the cobbler returns to being a cobbler and the tenor to being a tenor. Gramel picked these stories out of an ancient reader and got an assistant in the press office to write the dialogue. The proverb was not quoted, but had to be guessed from the action. Pössner crept quietly from the studio and went to the cloakroom to wash his face. It was a harmless cut on top of a bump on his forehead. Someone stuck plaster over it in the form of a cross. Gramel's secretary, who sat up in the control room beside her boss, came along to ask Pössner if he would be able to do his final piece. She told him that people were already ringing up, and Gramel thought it splendid how he was managing to carry on. Pössner returned to the studio.

Everybody there gave him encouraging nods and smiles, and some of them came up to whisper that today's program had everything and was bound to get him a lot of fan mail.

He went over to the schoolteacher, who was sitting on a bench at the side, watching him.

"Does it hurt?" she asked.

"Not really."

"If you make a cold poultice the bump will disappear."

"Are you leaving right after the show?"

"Right away. The bus trip takes a good two hours. The children must get home."

"But you would have time for a glass of beer with me?"

"I could manage time for a beer," she whispered.

Pössner went over to the curtain and took up his position.

"There we are," he said, as the red light on the camera lit up for him, "that was our third brainteaser, our third puzzle. Write your answers on a postcard and send it in to us. We shall put all the correct ones into a hat and draw lots to decide which of you will be invited to take part in our next program. I hope you've enjoyed yourselves. I myself have had a splendid time, and now I am going to put a cold poultice on this bump on my head. Good-by till next week."

As the closing music was being played Pössner made a bow, grinning slightly as he did so to show that the action was voluntary. Everyone kept still until the continuity girl had done her final announcements and apologized for a short transmission break in the area of Wachsenstein-Bingen.

The stage designer appeared at once on the platform. He held the metal clip up in the air and remonstrated with a carpenter, who however disclaimed all responsibility for it. The other carpenter who had been working the bulldozer from beneath also swore he was innocent. Pössner intervened, calling the stage designer a hopeless bungler. It had been a shitty bit of carelessness, it showed that you couldn't trust artists.

The designer swung the clip to and fro in silence.

Beaming, Gramel came into the studio. "We can be grateful," he said mildly. "The program was a great success. It could not have been more graphic and spontaneous. I thank you all."

And to Pössner he said, "That is the advantage of a live program. The viewer accepts it without question when things go wrong. You did very well. The telephone exchange has its hands full. Are you coming to the canteen?"

The young guests came to say good-by. Some of them were going off at once to the railway station, others had to be taken to the airport. Gramel's secretary had assumed this thankless task. The boys made their bows to Pössner, the girls curtsied— among them the fourteen-year-old, whom he regarded with a cold eye. Bibi, pale and subdued, stood silently by.

"Bibi, give my regards to your father. Tell him to keep it up in that workshop."

The little boy, swollen-eyed, did not reply, but held tight to the secretary's hand. Two mothers, who had brought their children from somewhere in the neighborhood, came up to thank Pössner. He bowed and gave them a brilliant smile. They were sturdy women in their best Sunday clothes, with rings on their fingers and proud necks rising up from bright-colored blouses. Pössner felt a sort of greedy respect for such women, who sat safely in their houses and had what they needed. He stole a glance at their firm buttocks, drawing folds across skirts through which the whalebones showed. They were well-covered, in splendid trim. A spasm of lust shot up his belly. He had visions of molestation and rape, saw them scream in quaking terror and rush up against him in sweet dread. All that came flooding over him as he made his bow and thanked them for bringing along their charming, attentive, and clever children.

After a program everybody goes off to the canteen. The first to go are the technicians, who position themselves at the tables in tight groups in the expectation of free rounds. They stick their heads together and smile superior smiles, but do not dare in so many words to remind the producer of his duty. With Gramel it is pointless anyway: his soft majesty has a damping effect on technicians.

But when Hügi is there brandy flows. Even before the performance he can be seen doling out bottles to the stagehands, to the technical operators, and to the people in white overalls on whom everything depends, though nobody knows exactly what they do.

Pössner took a seat among the drama students and at last got his beer. The first glass turned to steam in his throat, but the second, interspersed with sips of Doppelkorn, restored his spirits. "We should do a live program on camping in the Black Forest," he said, "and fry our own sausages."

The drama students laughed gratefully. They had been in front of the TV cameras. It was terrific, they thought, and so different from the stage. You mustn't turn your head an inch too much, mustn't raise your voice or make faces, must be sparing of gesture and intense, never relaxing your concentration. You can't get away with bluffing, the camera registered everything. They knew it all now, and confirmed it eagerly to one another.

A flock of ballet girls came in from the other studio where the rehearsal had just ended. They infiltrated the gaps at the tables but stayed together, some of them sharing chairs. They were thin girls with deep cavities around their collarbones and hectic horsy faces, wearing tight tricots with padded brassières.

As Pössner was on his fourth beer, nodding happily to all the conversations going on around him, the male dancers came in —slim men with swaying torsos and sharp noses. Invariably when these characters enter a room they start jerking their heads in all directions, looking for acquaintances. When they speak, they throw in words from various languages and finish practically every sentence with a bit of technical jargon, which can bear all sorts of meanings, some of them tenderly obscene.

It had become a custom for the program people to eat together after the performance—Gramel and his secretary, Markus Hügi, the puppetmaster, and Pössner. As a rule they went to an Italian restaurant, but sometimes to a Greek, Yugoslav, or French one. This time Pössner suggested a place in the old part of the town, where they served wonderfully juicy hamburgers. Hügi was reluctant. Grubby eating places, he said, played havoc with his digestion and reminded him of his spell of fever in Egypt when he was appearing in a circus. Since Gramel also pleaded an important engagement at the golf club, Pössner drove off home on his motor scooter.

Fired with beer and Doppelkorn, he took the curves with screeching tires, flogging his little engine till it screamed. Oh, for the freedom of the long-distance truck driver, the highway cavalier! That would be the life for him. Not here, of course, but way out in the steppes, on log roads, life preserver within reach, water bottle swinging from the dashboard, nights in a sleeping bag beneath the truck, with distant animals howling. Five days on the run, powerful, alone, his hands firm on the wheel. Oil-stained shirt stretched across his suntanned shoulders, he kisses his lucky charm, sweating, knowing what he wants, a man of few words. He bears a priceless load marked urgent, delivers it, and pockets the dough.

Arriving home, Pössner took a warm shower, then sat himself down in front of the telephone with a glass of red wine within reach. His parents lived in Diepoldsreuth, a little town in Bavaria. His mother answered the call.

"How was I?" he asked.

"We went to the Gasthof Engel again," his mother said, "and saw it on the set in the private room. You know the one I mean. They really are so kind, they opened it up specially for us. Oh dear, what a shock you gave us! It was a near thing, wasn't it? You might have been killed. We all screamed. My boy, we are all so proud of you. I don't know how you do it. I mean, how can you remember it all?"

"Then you liked it?"

"And then that sweet little boy! What an intelligent child!

Don't the children get terribly excited, being allowed to take part like that? If we had had television when you were small, I don't think I should have had a moment's peace. You were always so interested in new things."

"Did Grandma see it too?"

"No, not this time. She does interrupt so, and never stops asking questions. She just can't follow it properly. But I thought you were looking a bit thin. Are you sure you're getting enough sleep? Do you have a hot meal every day?"

"Yes, I sleep and eat enough," he said.

"Well, you know best, I suppose. But do please look after yourself. I know how it is, what with the city and such an interesting job. It's easy to lose your sense of proportion, you know—you mustn't give way to everything."

"Could you follow what I was saying when I was building that bulldozer?"

"Every word. It was so interesting. I know nothing at all about machines, as you know, but the way you do it—I'm learning a lot. People are sure to stop me again tomorrow when I go shopping. The Permuts have bought a television set especially because you appear on it. You know—the doctor who bought our building plot outside the town. It's quite understandable that a mother should be proud of her son, isn't it?"

"Of course it is. Give me Father quickly."

"Good luck, then, and think of us sometimes. Couldn't you come down next weekend?"

"It would be difficult. I have programs the next four Sundays."

"Give me a kiss," said his mother, and laughed.

Pössner made a kissing noise into the telephone and laughed too. Then his father was speaking.

"Congratulations, my boy, so your expensive education was not all wasted. You certainly put it across."

"Thanks," said Pössner. "It's only for children, I know. But one must start somewhere."

"That doesn't matter. You'll get there in time. I'm sure of that."

"Yes, I certainly will."

"Just one small thing I might mention," his father said. "It sometimes bothers me that you still speak with a slight accent. Now and again there's a Bavarian intonation as you end your words. Perhaps you should take elocution lessons. People have been spoiled by the theater into expecting every word to be pronounced correctly. As I say, it's only a small thing. You are my son, and so it is all the more important that I should try to be objective."

"I'm not an actor. A bit of dialect makes the program more personal."

"Whatever you say. It doesn't really worry me, it's just a suggestion," his father said. "Keep it up, my boy, work hard and come as soon as you can. We look forward to that. Good-by."

The apartment was clean and there was food to eat, but he didn't feel like reading and he could find nothing on the radio except a lecture and an operetta by Millöcker. He went out again.

The town, built on a series of hills, has fast roads with banked curves. The slope opposite the main station is kept as a municipal vineyard, but all the other hills are covered with houses with wrought-iron fences and rose-covered trellises in front of the windows. It is a wealthy city in a steamy bowl. In the winding valleys leading out from it there are elegant factories with plenty of glass and with frescoes on the walls. When Pössner was feeling good he would drive through the city, flitting between the cars, charging up the hills with open throttle, and whistling down the tarred ribbon on the other side. He would brake, lean over to the side, accelerate, cut off the engine, sitting upright and with his weight thrown forward on the very tip of the saddle, the wind billowing out his shirt and trousers. He wore an old hat, fixed with a rubber band under his chin.

The fastest road is made of concrete slabs laid over a river-bed, and it runs along the valley past the railway station through the industrial quarter. On the left are the cranes and silos of the canal docks, on the right the coal mounds of the electricity works, where coke is also made. On the gantries above the ovens little men can be seen hopping about and poking with prongs. Glowing coke slides down into the trucks beneath, drawing a slanting ribbon of fire across the night, and through the oven doors robes of flame flutter in the wind.

Pössner opened up the throttle, gripped the saddle tight between his thighs, and, taking his hands off the handlebars, rode along the arterial road beneath the orange light. At every jolt of the front fork on the tarred joints between the concrete slabs he would give way at the hips and slide forward. He got faster and more reckless. He started to sing. With slight movements of the shoulders he countered the wind pressure of passing cars. He rushed on, feeling on top of the world. Now and again he was assailed by sudden stenches—from the city slaughterhouse, a leather factory, and farther down the rubber works with its aura of burning fat. The valley opened out and became colder. Pössner put his hands back on the handlebars. The wind drew tears from his eyes and mucus from his nose.

After journeys such as this, with a few short drinks swallowed in bars along the way, Pössner usually spent the night with Rosi, his mistress of the moment. She was thin, determined, and worked to a schedule which called for a husband at thirty and a baby at thirty-one—preferably a boy. Rosi's father was managing director of a chocolate factory. She had a small apartment of her own and worked as a translator in a car factory. She would have a car of her own only when she could pay for it out of her wages.

She was holding a skirt over one arm and a clothesbrush in the other hand when she opened the door to Pössner.

"You should have given me a ring first," she said. "I've got nothing in the house."

"I am at peace with the world," he said. "Give me a brush too. I am at peace with the world, and therefore I am innocent."

"You're drunk."

"All I can reply to that is that you are not drunk. But even if you were, you red-headed doll, you would still be nowhere near at peace with the world."

"Do you want something to eat?"

"No, but still I'm at peace with the world, wrapped in bliss even when wielding a brush and spreading the dust of Sundays across your tiny skirt. My bliss is almighty and in splendid fettle. Indeed, I scarcely know what it is to know that you are not also at peace with the world."

"You are disgustingly drunk," she said.

"Does my breath smell?"

Still brushing the skirt over her arm, he followed her through the room, through the kitchen, into the bathroom and back into the room, breathing at her, belching out the sour gas from his stomach, head thrust forward on a puffy neck. He was laughing, asking her to tell him the truth, to smell his breath and judge dispassionately.

"Oh, you're the filthiest of pigs," she cried. "Go away, and never come near me again."

"I am not the filthiest of pigs," he said. "I have right on my side as long as I am at peace with the world."

"You are just horrible and vulgar."

"I have right on my side," he said, and seized her around the neck, massaging the nape. Gasping, she drummed on his chest, pinched him in the side with her long and powerful fingers. It hurt a lot and drove him on to work faster and harder, for the milky skin of her face was growing more transparent. They struggled together, he kneaded her back, pushed aside her knees, she punched him under the arm, he forced back her head, she pressed her lips together tight to hide the expectant smile at the corners of her mouth. And in the end they were both lying on the floor, fully roused, the table above them and his legs lashing against the edge of the sofa.

"Stop a moment," she said. "My watch is broken."

Pössner got to his knees and looked at her watch. The glass was smashed and the minute hand bent out of shape.

"I'll pay for it of course," he said. "I'll take it tomorrow to be repaired."

"It isn't worth much," she said. "My father gave it to me for Christmas. It's only plated."

"I've got a headache," Pössner said.

She made him a cold pack, and he sat back in the armchair, pressing the wet flannel against his forehead, while she cleared up, pulled out the studio couch, spread out the sheets, and made the bed.

"Feeling better?" she asked. "Shall I get you something to eat?"

She went into the kitchen and got undressed. Pössner seized the chance to get out of his clothes too. He quickly stuffed his none too clean underpants into the breast pocket of his jacket.

Before she joined him in bed she phoned the telephone exchange, kneeling naked on a dark red pouf at its head. She gave instructions to be called at half past six. When Pössner was there she did not trust her alarm clock.

Rosi's breakfasts were gorgeous. She brewed a green tea called Nordspitze, and on the table there were sardines, ham, honey, white bread, roasted almonds, cream cheese, pumpernickel, salami and eggs, but never butter. Pössner never asked himself why she always had these huge breakfasts on tap even when she was not expecting him. When he spent the night with Rosi, he was always in the office by nine and not, as usually happened, somewhere around eleven.

Gramel, who was in charge of all children's, women's, and teen-ager programs, made all the decisions himself. Whereas in other radio stations an editorial staff of twenty groaned over a similar amount of program time, Gramel, the gently indulgent chief, never gave the impression of working. He chatted on the phone, bought up films, farmed them out at cut rates for editing and synchronizing, scattered program suggestions among his script writers, while at the same time calmly dictating production details for a feature.

When Pössner, pale and haggard from lack of sleep, came into the office, Gramel was already deeply engaged with an elderly woman who was working on a cartoon series with a Biblical theme. It was to consist of ten installments, containing in all six hundred drawings. After five hundred the woman had lost her nerve: the woodcut heads of the disciples were becoming more knobby and the landscapes more and more dehydrated. Gramel was trying to make up the number of cartoons for the last installments by repeating some from the beginning. He also planned to pad out the narration and have some dramatic background music written. When Pössner came in, Gramel was stacking up the sheets of paper, numbering them in red pencil and putting Habakkuk from the third installment back again as Jacob in the tenth. The woman sat silent beside him.

At ten o'clock Markus Hügi came into the office, with cuffs down to his knuckles. He wanted an advance on his next program and was complaining because a stupid new doorman had refused to allow his red car into the courtyard. Gramel wrote him a chit for two thousand marks and sent him to the administration office for a second signature. After Hügi had gone, a twisted specimen from the library came in with the tapes of some jazzed-up folk songs which Pössner was supposed to listen to, to see if there was anything in them for his program. Then the secretary wanted him to help her go through the first two sacks of children's mail. He shouted "No," and did five quick push-ups. Then he thumbed through a hobbies periodical and rang up the stage designer, who was having trouble with the helicopter for the next program. Pössner wanted a decent helicopter with seats in the cabin for six children. There should be a handle inside to turn the rotor arms and a painted backcloth of clouds and signposts to heaven to add to the fun. The idea had been to give the illusion of flight by means of imperceptible movements of the camera and switching tricks, while the children waved through the portholes and looked downwards. Initial enthusiasm had now come down to groans and curses. The stage designer asked Pössner to send the hobbies paper across by messenger.

Finally Pössner sat down at a cutting desk two rooms farther on and watched films of a projected serial called "When I Was a Farmer's Boy." Each of the twenty-five installments had to be cut by three minutes. He set conscientiously to work.

The large building which the radio station had taken over after the war had previously housed the long-distance telephone exchange. A wing had been added later for the television offices. The studios had been built two streets away on a former sports ground. The restaurant was in the main building, its walls covered in brown trelliswork to give it a more intimate atmosphere.

Between ten and eleven the producers of programs for farmers come pushing through the door, large heavy men who sit down widely spaced at separate tables. A nod is enough to set the waitresses in motion, bringing them their beer, spirits, or nut milk. They are men of regular habits. They lean moodily over their glasses, swallowing their spit and suppressing anticipatory belches. Soon the food will come—greasy risotto or a thick soup with boiled bacon. The head of the newspaper cuttings office trips past them, collects his daily quantum of red wine from the buffet, and gambols out again. One after another the pachyderms rise to their feet and trudge to the john.

But the finest sights are to be seen during the lunch hour, when the restaurant fills up with brash commentators, narrators resplendent in sand-colored waistcoats, and carefully groomed secretaries. At one side two slim men sit apart, forks in their left hands poised over special diets and salads. They are producers of special TV features—only two or three a year, for they need time to prepare the ground. They travel about for weeks on end, inaccessible to all, walking straight as fir trees one behind the other along streets, or sitting modestly face to face with the great and famous. They put their questions coolly but precisely and snap their fingers behind their backs, but never at the same time. Splendidly attuned to one another, they wait till the lighting experts, the cameramen, and the sound engineers with their portable gear have done their work, till film has captured all the two of them have seen and suspected—and they see and suspect a lot. They are somebodies and really not a soul knows them. And that, you might say—and now they smile loftily and understandingly—is the hardest part of their work.

Who is not delighted to squeeze up when the program director, who does not eat like the members of the advisory board in the neighboring room, modestly begs for a corner of any handy table? He is a dark-suited youngster of middle age, who looks like a horseman but isn't. He is lean, filtered through rimless spectacles. Years ago nobody had heard of him, but he arrived one day and wriggled his way silently up to the top. He has no opinion but ironic memos for everybody, and no one can say that he is stupid. He is uncommitted and speaks with a carefully controlled accent. He is at all events on friendly though formal terms with the two TV critics, and they use each other's Christian names.

The broadcasting times of both radio and television go on far into the night, and during the evening the menus grow steadily longer and more select. One can have à la carte mussels with toast and salad, curd cheese spiced with herbs, pink slices of meat on a pretzel, or rare assortments of sliced sausage. A bachelor with a comfortable income—and there are quite a lot of them, in the light-entertainment department, for instance, or in the drama-script section—has to keep a careful watch on his waistline. They gather together, like with like, to feast, enliven the evening with wine, and tell tales to their protégés of the wild goings-on outside. These, permitted at last to see the restaurant for once from within, sit greedily absorbing the words which fall from the tables and probably contain the key to and the climate of success. At nearby tables sit people of both sexes chewing and drinking. These are actors, busy now with parts in radio plays after a whole morning spent kneeling on chalk marks and declaiming into cameras. Later still they will be standing on theater stages. They are always tired.

Far to the side, beneath the plate-sized light of a wicker lamp, sits the boss, the famous and infamous head of television plays. She is a professor and has hardly her equal in this majestic faculty. Everyone grumbles behind her back, but nobody draws the pistol that will shoot her to the ground. She sits alone. For a few minutes she thinks of nothing, savoring the overripe Romadour. With a fork she carefully presses the juice from a mound of radish salad, lets it slide over her tongue, opens wide her still maidenly gullet, swallows, and brings the frosted beer glass in a wide curve to her lips. In a moment a little round bubble of air will break free in her stomach and trip merrily upwards—to be expelled soundlessly through her nose. The head of drama has thin fair hair, wavy at the sides, a pointed nose, and rings of pale-colored stones on her fingers. Around her neck flutters a transparent mauve chiffon scarf, which she gathers up occasionally over the curved neckline of her dress. When she is finished she will pay out of a tiny soft leather purse, then, coming down on the accelerator, drive in second gear to the apartment house in which she has lived for years. The house shelters only four permanent guests in self-contained apartments. Such is the head of drama, whom nobody can shoot to the ground.

Pössner forced down his last sardine with the help of a piece of bread and tried again to fight back the awful images of assault, rape, and flagellation that flooded his mind. He was plunging his knife into a flabby female belly and using his fork to gouge the cochlea from diseased ears. A hideous force rose raging from his thighs and all but knocked against the base of the table. He drove home as fast as his scooter would allow, shut the window, and lay down on his bed. Sweeping everything aside, crushing and leaving bloody confusion behind him, he fought his way back to the sandbox and the gay-colored cake tins. He slept excellently.

On Tuesday the first letter was already on his desk. The schoolmistress wrote from Karlsruhe:

"Dear Herr Pössner—We have just started rehearsals on *A Man Who Called Himself Columbus*. I have written new words to the melody, so that the children will not know whom it is about and will have to guess from text and action that it is Columbus. I am not, however, clear in my mind whether Columbus should be already on land when he encounters the Indians, as envisaged by us, or whether we might not be able to show the ship first—that could be very picturesque—and then depict the meeting of the whites with the redskins, who assume a hostile attitude. Do please let me know at once what you feel, for we have of course only until Friday for rehearsals. Please give my regards to Herr Gramel. I am sorry that I was unable to come to the canteen on Sunday. The bus had to leave at once. I hope that you enjoyed your beer nonetheless. With best wishes, Yours—Annemarie Kaus."

Gramel's reaction to the letter was that Pössner should decide for himself, the main thing was that the play should last not longer than eight minutes—or nine at the outside. So Pössner wrote back by express mail, saying they must have the ship at all costs. Then he rang up the thin stage designer, who cursed him elaborately and said he did not have enough carpenters to build even the outlines of a sailing ship. He would just sling together a few packing cases and trail ropes from above: the rest he would get painted on a backcloth. That was his affair, Pössner said, and called him a bone-idle psychopath, which knocked the stage designer off his balance again.

On Wednesday morning Fräulein Kaus put through a call note from the school office. Pössner rang her back at once.

"Herr Pössner, I'm in difficulties," she said. "The Indians—the children are keen enough, of course, but I simply can't keep them in bounds. Things are getting out of hand. Couldn't you—? We are rehearsing again this afternoon."

"I'll be there," said Pössner. "I'll be right over."

"That will be wonderful. See you this afternoon."

"Get me a travel pass," Pössner shouted. "When does the train leave? What's the time now?"

Gramel's secretary dashed around, Pössner signed the travel pass, the train would leave in half an hour at noon exactly, Gramel signed the travel pass, Pössner borrowed some money from the secretary. Then he took a taxi to the station.

He got to Karlsruhe shortly before three. He had dozed in the hot upholstered compartment, had read a sporting paper and eaten two popsicles.

He rode in a taxi to the school, a red citadel of sandstone

blocks. He walked upstairs and looked at children's drawings hanging on the corridor walls. He saw a poster of a child with a ball running in front of a car. Happily he breathed in the dusty, urine smell of school and felt himself grown-up. He remembered that one afternoon shortly before his final examinations he had been going up just such a staircase as this. He had vowed then to remember that occasion when in adult years he would once again ascend a school staircase. Smiling, he entered the assembly hall.

Fräulein Kaus was leaning up against the grand piano, beating time on a gong, while Red Indians in bathing trunks and with chicken feathers in their hair danced around a group of sailors in ski boots. Georg, the class leader, shook Pössner by the hand and said it was magnificent that he had come along for the rehearsal.

Not very much remained to be done. The teacher had made a list of all the episodes and written in the margin beside them all position changes, entries and exits from the right and left, and the stopwatch time. In all, it came to something over eleven minutes.

The structure was sound, and all Pössner had to do was to shorten the various scenes. There was one girl in the cast, dressed up as a soothsayer, and she had to command the Indians to welcome the palefaces as friends. With this idea Fräulein Kaus had cleverly averted the danger of a fight.

The soothsayer was wrapped in a fringed tablecloth and had coral bracelets around her wrists. She was a skinny twelve-year-old, tall and thin. He told her to speak more slowly, but he could see by the way she turned her small moist face up to him that she wasn't listening. He had to take hold of her and place her in the right position.

Fräulein Kaus murmured to him that the soothsayer could be replaced by a medicine man—she had another boy in the second group who would be delighted to take over. Pössner replied that a girl among all those boys provided variety. The teacher pointed out that the girl was still very young and got too much absorbed in the action.

"Do you want to do this part?" Pössner asked the girl aloud.

The soothsayer nodded.

"Don't let them push you around, then. You're a soothsayer, and miles above all these men who are shouting their heads off and spoiling for a fight. But they obey your every word. Or don't you?" he asked aggressively, turning to the boys. "You muttonheads, you're just Indians, and have to do your war dance. But the soothsayer's a woman, and that's something quite different."

If that was how Herr Pössner saw it, Georg observed, then probably he was right. He had the most television experience.

"I'll say I have," Pössner replied. "And now let's take it again from the beginning."

Fräulein Kaus beat energetically on the drum, keeping the play on the move. Columbus scarcely had time to look through his telescope and spy land before she was there with her recorder, hustling the Indians into a war dance. Over the peace prophecy that followed she shook her head, and gave the cue a little early, so that Columbus and his sailors were standing too far off to exchange ceremonious handshakes with the Indians. At the end the soothsayer declared that in time to come this newly discovered land would be known as America, which was intended to be a joke and at the same time the answer to the problem.

"That's fine," Pössner called out and held up his stopwatch. "Seven minutes fifty seconds. All of you take note of your positions, we've finished now. We meet again on Saturday morning for the camera rehearsal."

The children did not move.

"What's the matter?"

"We don't know it properly yet," said the class leader.

"It'll come," said Pössner. "I see it all. Now off you go. Rehearsal's over."

They filed slowly out and down the stairs to their classroom to change.

The girl stayed behind and peeled off the fringed cloth. Pössner now saw clearly that her face and arms were painted dark brown.

"Gretel," the teacher said, "you must wait till the classroom is empty, then you can wash yourself downstairs."

"Let's go," he said. "What would you say to a coffee?"

"Fine—I'm dying for one."

As they walked slowly in the direction of the railway station they were overtaken by a succession of Red Indians and sailors on bicycles, ringing their bells long before they drew level and then calling out a greeting as they passed.

Outside the Zoo, where there was also a men's fashion store, were two cafés. One of them had canopied swing seats in front of the tables, the other and better one had palms in tubs. They could not make up their minds which to choose, for Fräulein Kaus seemed to remember that the iced coffee in the better café was too expensive, while the other place did not serve it at all.

"How much do you make?" Pössner asked her, smiling.

She had just bought a studio couch, and money was consequently a bit tight. They forgot coffee and ice and went into the Zoo, past the huge aviaries, the monkey hill, the zebra, gnu, and antelope enclosure, and the elephants' trampling ground, and came eventually to the little hill raised with rubble, which was covered with bushes and had benches along its winding paths. Fräulein Kaus was talking all the time.

She had taught at an elementary school in Mannheim before being transferred to Karlsruhe. She liked the class she had been given. They were lively children—a few rowdies and bullies among them, but she knew how to handle those. And not many girls—they are more boring than boys. Quite by chance she had been watching television at a colleague's home—she couldn't remember what the program was, it had been on a Saturday afternoon—but anyway she had enjoyed the children's play, and it had not taken long for her to make up her mind to try something similar herself.

"My last Christmas play in Mannheim was quite a success," she said. "It lasted one and a half hours. My three kings of

Orient were a bricklayer, a chimney sweep, and a gas-station attendant from different European countries. After all, they are supposed to have come a long way. The parents seemed to find it a bit confusing, but the children loved it and acted their heads off. You can't talk to modern children in terms of kings, I find."

"What about the text?" Pössner asked. "Everything just as if it were happening today?"

"Of course. I took an old Christmas play and simply transposed the characters. The way they talked grew quite naturally out of the situation. My chimney sweep was a fat boy with glasses, and as a tribute to the infant Jesus he did a handstand in front of the crib. The PT instructor was amazed. The crib, by the way, was a plastic bowl, since Mary and Joseph were camping during their flight. I didn't know the boy was going to do it: he had practiced it secretly at home."

They had left the Zoo by a side gate and were now in a quieter district of old houses.

"But you mustn't think," she said, "that it's all roses."

"I can believe that. Your colleagues?"

"The headmaster in particular. He's jealous. Television, you understand. He thinks the children might get spoiled."

"And what do you think?"

"I don't," she said. "We will finish the series, and that will be that. The children will forget all about it. They'll play football, and be just as good or as bad in school as they ever were."

"The bit of money the children get from us can hardly spoil them," Pössner said. "Five marks and a bottle of coke."

"The headmaster knows that. In any case the school gets four hundred marks for each program."

"As much as that? Gramel never told me."

"And how much do you get?" she asked with a smile.

"Double."

"I'm sorry," she said. "I was only joking."

"No, no, not at all. After all, you work on it more than I do."

Pössner caught sight of the time on a clock in one of the shops. He had missed his train. Fräulein Kaus begged his pardon for having kept him so long. Pössner told her not to worry —there was sure to be another train later. What he would like most of all now would be to have supper in her apartment.

He took her by the arm and said, "Okay?"

She nodded. He rushed into the nearest delicatessen shop and bought a bagful of marinated fish, various salads, and fruit.

The apartment consisted of a bed-sitting-room and kitchen. On the window sills potted plants stood beside a collection of cactuses, and the walls were hung with silhouettes and raffia work. The room was a bit cramped, since besides the armchair, wardrobe, and new studio couch a family dining table with four chairs took up a lot of space. Pössner found it very congenial— it had its own particular aura of a good family background combined with decency. He examined all the homemade things in it, among them an etching and a brass ashtray.

Fräulein Kaus gave a laugh. She had a typical schoolteacher's taste, she said. No doubt his own room was far more elegantly furnished. Pössner protested that everything was just right, and he was not going to stir from the room until they had eaten up all the fish and the salads.

She took the things from the delicatessen bag and put them out on small plates. She lit a candle and poured tea. Pössner sat in the armchair, she on the couch, ready to spring up at a hint to fetch a fork, a spoon, celery salt, or cranberry jelly from the kitchen.

"Living alone is not so bad when you're not at a loss for things to do," she said. "That's obvious. I never have enough time."

"Sometimes I don't get to bed before midnight for weeks on end," he said. "I have to keep an eye on the technical things too, though I know nothing about them."

But it must be an interesting job, she observed.

"It's interesting enough, but you must have a line of your own, otherwise you get swallowed up."

She could understand that, she said. It was on account of her new methods that she too had managed to gain attention. Pössner had risen and sat down beside her on the couch. He began to play with her fingers while she went on talking. Then she started to squeeze his fingers, but stopped at once when the doorbell rang.

"Who could that be?" she said, her hand still on his.

"Perhaps one of your colleagues," he suggested.

"At this time? Here at home? But I can't possibly answer."

The bell rang again, twice in succession. He drew his hand out from under hers and went to open the door. A troop of Indians and sailors in civilian clothes stood outside.

"Good that you're still here," said class leader Georg. "We wanted to say we're not at all happy about Gretel—the soothsayer."

"What's that?"

Pössner let the boys in, and they streamed into the little room as the teacher cleared away the remains of the food and disappeared into the kitchen. The children chatted among themselves and laughed when one got caught among the cactuses.

"Well, what is it?" Pössner asked loudly at last. "You can't just come pushing in, disturbing people like this."

"No, no, you're not disturbing," Fräulein Kaus called, coming out from the kitchen. "Have you had some new ideas? Oh dear, there's no room here for you all. You'd better sit on the table."

"We all think Gretel stinks," Georg said. "Anyway, soothsayers are something out of fairy tales, which the Red Indians didn't have. We've thought of another way of doing it. But it'll mean a battle."

The others all nodded.

"You can't have a battle," Pössner said. "You've got to be wrestlers and acrobats to make that effective. Viewers know too much these days. You didn't need to come here just for that."

Fräulein Kaus pointed out that some of the class had good marks for gymnastics. She was flitting about, moving cactuses out of the way and distributing cookies. Pössner looked at her.

"That's nonsense," he said. "The soothsayer stays."

The teacher glanced across at Pössner, who was standing beside the door and had nowhere to sit, since there were children everywhere. She was about to say something, but her attention was diverted by a boy who was trying to toast his cookie in the candle flame. The biggest boy of the class—the one playing Columbus—had brought along a dark red velvet bonnet with a yellow tassel. He wanted to know if he could use it for the broadcast. Another showed Pössner a bundle of red and green dyed feathers, and asked if he could make himself a headpiece out of them with a train down to the ground.

Pössner said yes to everything, though red and green are bad colors for television—they come out black on the screen. The children ought to be running off home now, he suggested.

"It's not so late," the teacher said. "Is there anything else you want to discuss? I hope you've told your parents you're rehearsing for television. Herr Pössner has made a special journey to Karlsruhe, and we don't want to disgrace him. Do you still know your words?"

The children began to run through Columbus from the beginning. They were slow and halting at first, since they were sitting in groupings different from those they knew on the stage. They stood up, sorted themselves into Indians and sailors, and were soon back in the swing. The teacher assumed the role of the missing soothsayer.

Now that the sofa was empty Pössner could sit down again. The children stood in a solid bunch in front of him. He could see only their backs, and there was nowhere to put his legs. The charade was going splendidly, he said. That would do.

After the second run-through he decided it was time to go. Standing at the door, he held the teacher's hand and asked her if she was satisfied now. Television seemed to have spoiled him, she said, and drew away her hand.

The children left with him and accompanied him to the station. The whole time, while he was still wondering whether to turn back and while he was waiting at the station for the train to arrive, they kept talking about Columbus.

Forest Park Cemetery

I still needed flowers. I paid for the sausages and the schnapps and walked across the road to the main entrance of the cemetery. It was one o'clock. The funeral would begin in half an hour.

I like cemeteries. They are not as crowded as the parks. This one was new to me. It was called the Forest Park Cemetery. Everywhere there are trees with soft needles smelling like bath salts, and I went to one and crushed a little twig in my hand. A sticky gum came out. It must have been an imported tree. The Forest Park Cemetery is our prettiest cemetery.

Although there was a lot of traffic on the street, it was quiet inside the walls. Or perhaps I was only imagining that in a cemetery it is always quiet. I'm never much good at things like that. And in any case I was thinking that it was on account of the funeral that I didn't have to work today. I wandered around the broad paths, smoking. And then I came to the chapel where the funeral services are held.

The corpses lay in their coffins in a high-ceilinged corridor. They lay behind glass on sloping ramps so that one could take a proper look at them. Little evergreen trees stood around them, and the wreaths were piled up beneath. In front of the dividing panels were handrails for the mourners. The corpses all looked old and peaceful. I was surprised to see what naturally earnest expressions dead people wear on their faces, but that is probably because when they are put in the chapel they have already been dead a couple of days. They were well and truly dead, and a bit made up. One old girl had red cheeks as if she had only just been roused to a state of excitement.

I read the names on the plates. My mother-in-law's was not among them: she had already been taken away. I saw none of my own people, only an undersized man who looked vaguely familiar. I went outside and sat down on a bench.

My mother-in-law was the true mother of my divorced wife, who was her illegitimate child. But my wife had been brought up by a foster mother who does not live in this neighborhood. My wife and her real mother had come together again by chance some years ago. And now she was dead. Some illness which had not been noticeable. I had never noticed anything, for my mother-in-law had always been a very lively person. I had once spent a night at her house, when things were going badly with me. By that time I was already divorced. That was the reason I was attending her funeral.

They were coming down the path toward the chapel: in front my wife in black with blonde hair. She was wearing sunglasses and looked very nice. Behind her came her stout friend and her friend's father, who is a golfer, I believe. Then came little Isolde, who had been with my wife at the time we were still married. I stood up and went to meet them.

"I'm glad you came," my wife said, and began to weep. "It is terrible."

I shook hands with the others and then fell in beside Isolde. She too was dressed in black and had an elaborate hairdo.

"It is terrible," she said. "I never even met her."

"How are things with you?" I asked.

"Fine. I've got a new job, with Infratest—that's a public opinion testing service. I have excellent prospects, and it's interesting work. But I have to get up very early, which I find a strain. And you? Did you come by streetcar? We've got heaps to tell each other."

We went into the mortuary.

"That's Kurt," Isolde said. "He was your mother-in-law's boy friend. He's been married for two years, but he was always with her."

My wife went across to Kurt and embraced him. They stood in front of the window with its empty bier and wept together.

They looked to me like a married couple. An attendant came out from behind a holly tree, bowed, and then pulled the curtains shut. Things were beginning to move.

Some more women had arrived in the meantime—friends of my mother-in-law. Large women, all tensed up.

Inside the chapel I did not know where to go, for there was nothing in it except a few chairs, on which my wife's stout friend Luise, her father, and the other fat women sat down. So I positioned myself behind my wife and little Isolde. It was like old times.

"Have you got a handkerchief?" my wife said. "The organ's starting."

I hadn't got one, but Kurt had. So I changed places with him and sat down on his chair.

The hall was cool and had mosaics on the ceiling. It looked like the inside of a war memorial. It had been cleverly done, for it had to be used by all denominations.

Suddenly from somewhere above came the sound of music. Organ, violin, and a man singing. In the empty hall it sounded very solemn. Four attendants came in pushing the coffin on rubber-tired wheels. Behind it came the priest. Now little Isolde was crying too.

The music kept on for a long time. It gave the women time for weeping: after all, that's what it was for. The priest looked down at his book and waited quietly. I was surprised that the cemetery attendants looked so sad, when they have nothing at all to do with the corpses they look after. But probably their suitability for their jobs lies precisely in the fact that they can look sad without being involved. Their work is not easy, and demands a certain skill.

I turned around once to look at my wife. She had her sunglasses on and was crying into the handkerchief. She stood on her high heels leaning slightly forward, the right hip turned in, which gave the appearance of voluptuous grief.

Then the priest said something vague to the effect that the dead woman was dead. His receding hair reminded me of the studied virility of television news reporters. "Now let us accompany Frau Klara Pasch to her last resting place," he said, and led the way out.

We formed up behind the coffin. My wife was at the front with Kurt, then came Isolde and myself, Luise with her father, and behind them the other women. Bells were ringing, of course.

The main paths of cemeteries are always lined with the graves of famous people. I looked at obelisks, boulders, and sarcophagi. I had not known that so many famous people were dead, or rather that so many dead people were famous. Most of them I had never heard of. I asked little Isolde. She wanted to make me laugh and said each time that this one had been a general or a composer. They were all men, I noticed. Women don't get large tombstones so easily.

We turned off to the left. The trees became higher and the graves closer. As we went past, people moved aside and turned back to look at us. In front the coffin glided along on rubber tires. I thought of my mother-in-law lying inside, broad hips supported on glossy paper cushions, flesh wobbling ceaselessly. It was unimaginable that she would sit up or speak. That's how one thinks of it as a child, and then gets a shock when for the first time, perhaps during the war, one sees dead men falling into ditches or being loaded onto trucks. I tried to bring my mother-in-law back to life in my mind. I thought of her sitting behind wine bottles, telling jokes, and slapping her thighs so vigorously that her dressing gown burst open. But it was no good. I knew that she was dead and lying in her coffin, that's the way it was. Even the most potent method I know of for making me think of a woman failed me this time.

The grave lay on the edge of a field in new plots, behind the farthest hedge of the cemetery. The attendants placed the coffin on belts and let it down. Kurt and my wife were crying again.

" 'Go to now,' " the priest began, " 'ye that say today or tomorrow we will go into such a city, and continue there a year, and buy and sell and get gain. Whereas ye know not what shall be on the morrow. For what is your life? It is even a vapor, that appeareth for a little time and then vanisheth away.' James, Chapter Four, verses 13 and 14. No different was the life of our departed sister. No one thought—and least of all she herself—that she would die so swiftly. Our petty human understanding may feel that it was too late for repentance, yet all of us are dependent on God's infinite mercy. For guilt belongs not to the deceased alone, but also perhaps to those she leaves behind."

Kurt gave a sob. My wife held herself upright, proud no doubt of being thus under attack.

"She was abandoned by all, and she died in sin. Modern life is merciless, whether in work or in leisure. Those who are not sustained by love can easily be overwhelmed. Klara Pasch gave much love and received little. But Jesus Christ died for her as well."

At this moment an elderly woman pushed forward and gave Kurt a sharp blow in the back.

"You filthy swine," she shouted. "Aren't you ashamed? First the mother, and now the daughter. You bastard, you should be struck dead on the spot. Adulterer!"

She kept on hitting and pulling at Kurt's sleeve, who shook his shoulders after each blow. My wife moved a few paces to the side and put on her sunglasses. We all of us made room for Kurt and the elderly woman. Even the priest and the attendants drew back.

"Think of your wife and children. Have you no shame, you filthy swine? It's them you belong to—not to her there. You pig, you filthy swine, you—"

Kurt turned and struck her in the face. The woman stumbled but recovered at once and screamed, "Murderer! Adulterer! He should be put in jail."

"I'll kill you, you bitch," Kurt shouted. "My memories are sacred to me. I'll shut you up—shut you up for good!"

My wife's stout friend Luise and I sprang forward and got hold of Kurt just in time to stop him from seizing the woman by the throat. Luise clamped his head beneath her arm while I tried to grab his hands. But Kurt was so strong that I was knocked aside and Luise was dragged forward, though she braced her feet against the floor.

"I'll kill her! I'll kill her!"

"Filthy swine," the woman screamed from farther down the path. "Adulterer!"

"I'll kill her!"

Behind us someone was calling for the police. As Kurt swung us around in circles I saw that my wife and little Isolde were standing clasped in each other's arms. They both had their sunglasses on, and under them the tears were streaming down. Knowing them both as I do, I could see that they were also laughing. I did not see the priest.

Luise, who runs a chicken grill and knows how to deal with rabid men, quelled Kurt. She spoke earnestly with him and then led him off along a side path toward the exit gates. The rest of us followed at a respectable distance.

"To wreck my devotions like that," Kurt was sobbing. "The bitch, she's just jealous. She's a one to talk. When she's got a child by another man and was always with him—with a husband in the war. Now both of them are dead, and she's got nobody left. She'd hate to see anybody happy."

"Then why worry?" Luise said.

The cars were standing in front of the cemetery. We divided ourselves between Luise's sports car and her father's sedan. Kurt did not want to come, but my wife persuaded him. Everybody lit cigarettes, and we drove off.

My wife and little Isolde live with Luise and her father. They pay neither rent nor board, and each has a room of her own. Luise is away at her chicken grill during the week and only comes home for weekends. So my wife has Luise's room. The father doesn't object. His wife is no longer living, and Luise is his only daughter.

Luise is very efficient. The table was already set for coffee. But before we sat down we all had to drink a schnapps.

"It'll make us feel better," Luise said and patted Kurt on the shoulder. But Kurt still had tears in his eyes for a long time after that.

"God is my witness, I loved her, only her. She was everything to me. Ten years we were together. Sonia can confirm it."

My wife nodded and drank a schnapps. "Don't get sentimental. Maybe you are a married man, but my mother was always fond of you. She hadn't anyone else, not even me."

She stood up and went out.

"Since her mother died," Luise said to me, "she's been reproaching herself for being a bad daughter. She cried for two whole nights. I could do nothing. And this morning she made me drive into town to buy her a New Testament. That's the way it goes—you only realize the wrong you've done when it's all over."

"Yes," said Kurt.

"You did everything right," Luise addressed him. "When you're fond of somebody, nobody has a right to reproach you."

"I really was fond of her, and I'll prove it, whether people like it or not. I'll give Klara the finest tombstone on the market, even if I have to work five solid years to pay for it."

My wife came back with two little kittens in her arms. "Here's Peter and Hilde. Aren't they sweet? They've just been eating a bit of liver. Imagine."

"Two-week-old cats don't eat meat," Luise replied.

"Liver they do."

"Not liver either."

"But I saw it with my own eyes! Little tiny pieces from my hand. Just look at those sweet little tongues!"

"Two-week-old cats only drink milk."

Luise's father laughed. He was sitting at the head of the coffee table, holding his cup in his hand. We all looked at him. He put the cup down again and took a piece of cake.

"Cats have far more pride than human beings," my wife said. "Little Hilde is already a real young lady. She snuggles up and makes eyes, but only when it suits her. Yesterday she would have nothing to do with me at all. She wouldn't even eat out of my hand. With people, as long as you're nice to them and give them something now and again, they're quite happy. Most don't even get that much."

I got a nudge on the leg. Little Isolde gave me a sideways wink.

"How old was she really—your mother?" I said.

"Forty-seven. I was born when she was nineteen. She was a nurse in a children's home. Her father was a framemaker in a furniture factory. My mother told me once that he often came home drunk, and then would start beating his wife. The whole family—three girls and a boy—lived in a single room with a kitchen. And when the drunken brute had done hitting, he would take her behind the bed curtain. The children had to hear it all. My mother never forgot that."

"You told the story better last time," said little Isolde. "On that occasion you all had only a kitchen to live in, and your grandfather was a Communist deputy."

"Funny, aren't you?" my wife said. "If you don't believe me, ask him yourself. I can show you pictures. He lives in Hanover with his second wife. They've been there a year and are doing fine; they got away from Berlin just in time. Anyway, I'm not blaming my grandfather. He's as God made him. I just wanted to make the point that my mother didn't have an easy childhood."

"Kurt, help yourself to cake," said Luise.

He didn't want to, but since Luise had called him by his Christian name, he let himself be helped to some gingerbread.

"Tell us more," I said.

"You know it all already."

"I always like to hear it again, and there's nobody to contradict you now."

"No one knew Klara as well as I did," said Kurt. "Before she died she made me a sign."

"No, it was me she made a sign to," my wife said.

Kurt gave a sob and shook his head.

"She meant both of you," Luise said.

"Nonsense," said my wife. "I was with her the whole of the

last day. She lay in the oxygen tent and smiled at me before she lost consciousness. I know my own mother, don't I? 'Stop blubbering,' she whispered. I could scarcely hear her, she was so weak. And then she came around for the last time. I can see her now, how she struggled to raise her arm and tried to say something—"

"She was praying," said Kurt. "Nobody dies without praying. My mother died with the holy sacraments."

"Your mother, but not my mother. She didn't need them. She was far too gay for that."

"Like you," said little Isolde.

"Stop bickering," said Luise. "Who wants more coffee or tea?"

"Me, please," said her father. "Our mother lay a whole year in bed with dropsy before she died, isn't that so, Luise?"

Luise nodded and refilled his cup.

"My mother was happy when she got that job as a student nurse in the children's home," my wife went on. "She had her own bed, enough to eat, and interesting work."

"Are children interesting?" asked little Isolde.

"To me they are," I said, "since I have none."

"But not to the daughter of a framemaker."

"Is that meant as a reproach?" my wife asked.

"What else?"

"We're not married now," she said, "but for five years we were. Let me go on telling you about my mother."

"You mean, about your idea of your mother. But what's the point, anyway? She's dead."

"I know she's dead," my wife shouted. "But if I did everything wrong, at least I want to talk about it. Does anyone object?" She gave a sob and slumped over the table.

"Yes, I do," said little Isolde. "You start showing off as soon as you open your mouth."

Luise wanted to say something, but little Isolde waved her down so violently that Luise, being unused to it, was surprised into silence.

"I know you inside out. No doubt you told the priest how

badly you treated your mother and how guilty you feel and how everyone must pay sometime for her lack of consideration and her laziness, and how it serves you right to have a dead mother on your hands."

"And what if I did? What does it matter to you?"

"I'll tell you exactly. It matters because your mother didn't die so that you could wallow in a guilty conscience. Your mother was ill, and that had nothing at all to do with you."

"And now let me tell you something. When I feel bad about anything, it does something to me, it makes a new person of me. Every religion preaches that."

I thought of the New Testament which she all of a sudden wanted to read, and I had to admire her. She was miles ahead of us all in the art of choosing a line and sticking to it.

"I loved her and will love her for the rest of my life," Kurt said loudly. "She was the best woman on earth. Anyone who says a word against her will have me to deal with."

"Shut up, you stupid fool."

"Then you be quiet too," I had to put in. "His tears mean just as much as your tears. Don't think there's any difference."

"For her there is," little Isolde whispered. "She knows tears make her attractive."

Luise's father stood up. "Please excuse me," he said. "I have to leave. I'll be back in an hour." And off he went.

"You can go too," my wife screamed at me. "You know me only too well, don't you? I'm superficial and frivolous. I deserted you, and I bring misery to everybody."

"You're just lazy, that's all."

"All right," she said. "Somebody has got to suffer."

"Does anyone still want coffee?" Luise said. "Otherwise I'll clear up. We'll be having supper soon."

"Stay where you are," my wife said. "It's my turn now. You can get supper later."

Unperturbed, Luise piled up the crockery on a tray and went out. She came back to fetch the other things.

I was beginning to get bored, for I hadn't planned to spend

the whole of my free day on the funeral. As I stood up, little Isolde signed to me with her cigarette to stay where I was.

"You needn't stay," my wife said. "We're no longer married."

"He'll stay for supper," Luise declared. "That's only right at a funeral."

I stayed, of course. When a man like me is told categorically what he should do, he does it. I am not particularly weak—simply irresolute. Maybe I have no spirit.

"He was only twenty," my wife began again. "She met him on her second day off. That was a big occasion for her, because during the first six months she wasn't even allowed out of the place. She came of an underprivileged family with asocial habits, after all. His father was a rich man. She fell for the boy at once, and he knocked her up. As he was so young, it was natural that he should want to marry her. But his father had other ideas."

"Do you know your father?" asked little Isolde.

"Yes, she knows him," I said. "He's the pride of the family and has something to do with East-West trade. You see his name in the papers sometimes."

"Something like that. My husband always gets spiteful about people who earn a lot of money. He thinks they're all stupid."

"Not any more. I earn money now too."

"And what happened with your mother?" Luise said.

"She gave birth to her child, and six weeks later was thrown out of the children's home."

"So you're a pauper's daughter," said little Isolde.

"You shouldn't poke fun at dead people." Kurt had leaped to his feet, a fork in his hand. "If a man got Klara into trouble, that was his fault, not hers."

"Nobody's blaming her. And anyway I meant Sonia." Little Isolde gurgled. She took off her glasses and looked at Kurt with the expression of an intelligent child—much too young for her age. I like her when she peers in helpless shortsightedness in one particular direction, just about able to make something out. "I think it's marvelous for a nurse in a children's home to give birth to a child."

"Of course," said Luise. "You always think it's marvelous when other people do the living and you can just stand and look on. As long as it doesn't affect you, there's no harm in talking about it, is there? Look at you: twenty-six years old and still no steady man! These days—and for a person of your intelligence—that's positively indecent. I suppose you think it's enough to lie in bed now and again with a man much older than yourself and rub up against him, just because you don't have to feel ashamed of yourself. You act the innocent little girl so he thinks you're eighteen, and then he won't get rough with you, or he'll want to have you for keeps. You get out of everything."

"And what about you?" little Isolde said. "What do you do?"

"Well, at least I'm unhappy. But that's something you know nothing about either. I know that I gave up too soon, just because the first man I had anything to do with didn't handle me right. Just look at me: I'm made for having five children and driving a tractor. And what have I got? A chicken grill and a girl friend using my money to get a rest from a messed-up marriage and a few messed-up love affairs. And the awful thing is I don't even mind that she just barely puts up with me."

"I didn't know you were so unhappy," my wife said to her.

I could tell from her voice that it was a matter of complete indifference to her how unhappy Luise was. She had her mother's death and her guilty conscience, and was in no hurry to let them go.

"Do you want me to leave?"

"You'll leave all right when you can't stand it any longer," Luise said. "As long as that lasts I'll go on paying. People like you are all I can expect now."

I felt I must go over to Kurt and clink glasses with him. He stood up for it. At this moment I felt really fond of him, for he had not understood a word Luise was saying. My wife was smoking, little Isolde lighting up again, and Luise picking at crumbs on the table. It was now too late for me to go away.

We were all of us ordinary decent people. Particularly Kurt.

During the day he repaired cars in a garage, and for eight years he had sat out his evenings with Klara Pasch, had drunk wine with her, played checkers, and loved her. That night I had spent at her house she told me she had got used to having Kurt around: he was young, stupid, and good-natured. Now and again she slept with another man. When he found out, he would hit her. That was all right; for him there was no other way of forgiving. All the rest of us, and particularly her daughter, could go to hell as far as she was concerned. We were good at talking our way around our feelings. Kurt was honest and was there when she wanted him, and that was the important thing.

When Kurt got the cashier of his garage with child on a company picnic, he married her. It took him a long time to get over the fact that his Klara raised no objection. He thought she wanted to get rid of him. However, my mother-in-law was magnanimous and kept him on. He could have his family, but the rest belonged to her. She was getting older, and at times he was too violent for her. When I've had enough, she told me, his wife can have the whole business. That way she's got something to look forward to. A bit of jealousy is good for a woman, otherwise she lets herself go and runs to fat. She laughed and took another bite at her sausage. Yes, I know, but on me it's attractive. Anyway, I don't get the thrill out of it I used to twenty years ago.

As I said, I slept with her only once. But the only thing I can remember about it was the breakfast.

My wife started to talk again. It's wonderful the way she can ignore things.

"My mother never went on the streets. She took a few lovers over the years, for after all she had a child to bring up. But then she turned me over to a childless couple who later adopted me. They're both still alive, though I never see them now. My mother was in auxiliary service during the war. She traveled all over Europe, learned to type and to look after accounts and was always surrounded by men. I've got pictures of that time, and she really looks lovely—with a wave of hair half over her face. Then in a village in France she met an officer. He was an educated man and very good-looking. He was already thirty-five, but the first time they slept together she found out that he had never slept with a woman before. After that she couldn't help falling in love with him. After the war, they set up house together, and it wasn't until six years later that she discovered he had belonged to a Catholic order and had left it on her account. From then on she worshiped him. And was unfaithful to him when she couldn't put up any more with just worshiping him. There were times when she couldn't bear it: he was simply too good for her.

"I called him Uncle Philip. I was fifteen when I first met him. My mother used to wait for me outside the house where I was living with my foster parents, and she kept on at me until in the end she convinced me that she was really my mother. She looked very smart with that long wave. Of course, for me it was all much more exciting than my foster parents at home. And when I was seventeen I ran away from them.

"In the end Uncle Philip left my mother. After that she married a salesman, but it only lasted for two years. He was a diabetic. Then she moved here. Uncle Philip is still alive. He went back again to his monastery. They had to take him back: he was too valuable to them. And now he's one of their top men, in charge of all the Catholic missionaries in Africa."

"We looked him up on our honeymoon," I said. "He's very intelligent-looking and two heads taller than me. He even had a meal with us. Afterwards he took me aside and slipped a hundred-mark note into my hand."

"Mine too," my wife said, "but I never told you."

"What did you do with the money?"

"Bought cosmetics and a couple of blouses."

"I never noticed."

She smiled. To me that means danger, for she can look at you so sweetly that you automatically think all's well and become overconfident. But in fact her smile means nothing.

"I must stretch my legs," I said, "or I won't be able to manage supper."

There was a little garden at the back of the house. Kurt and my wife followed me out. The garden was rather neglected, and there were twigs and an old torn mattress lying about in it.

"The kittens play about with that," my wife said. "They build themselves nests. Yesterday their mother brought them a piece of a mouse."

"That was mean, what you said about your mother," Kurt said. "She was a decent woman."

"Kurt," she said, smiling, "of course she was a decent woman, because she was fond of all the men she lived with. And what more can a woman want? I don't really blame her for handing me over to someone else when I was a child. She was still too young."

"She was right when she said you had no conscience. You tried to get me once, and only because you begrudged me to your mother. You enjoy getting a rise out of other people."

"Yes, so I do. I'm superficial, so I've got a bigger appetite. I'm like my mother."

"The hell you are! She helped me and was good to me. I shall never forget her."

"I won't either," my wife said.

Kurt kicked a stone against the fence and went back indoors. I could see him helping Luise set the table.

From the window above, little Isolde warbled down to us. "Do you mind if I change my clothes? There's a big stain on my black jacket." She slammed the window shut.

I took a close look at my wife. She had got older. Her hair was in good shape, but too bleached for my taste. It made her face look puffy. And the flesh around her neck was no longer firm. She was getting more and more like her mother. Nice long legs, but for her five-foot-eleven she was twenty pounds too heavy. Which can be attractive, of course, in a maternal sort of way, though perhaps it only works like that on me because I'm two inches shorter than she is. That's not just a complex of mine. One can in fact be rougher, that is to say more shameless, with large women. And of course it's a bigger exertion.

"And what about you? What have you got to reproach me with?"

"Nothing," I said.

"Have you got a girl friend?"

"Not a regular one."

"And so you're content?"

"Maybe even happy."

"You don't have to share your money any more."

"That too," I said. "I give only when I want to give. That's pleasant and convenient."

"Yes, it's doing you good," she said. "I was something of a strain on you."

"I was too young. And much too serious."

"That was flattering for me."

"To begin with. Then you got bored."

"What are you doing now?"

"I'm secretary to a man who owns a newspaper and a small savings bank. It's the first job I've had that I like. I handle the telephone, make appointments, head people off—"

"But you know nothing about running newspapers or banks."

"That's just why he took me on. Because I had done so many different jobs and wasn't specialized. You are gifted, he told me, and you're not set in your ways. And that's exactly what I need."

"You're exaggerating! Be honest, now. You're really nothing but a sort of glorified chauffeur."

I couldn't help laughing. "No, I'm a secretary. I don't work on his newspaper, nor in his bank. I just sit around in his office listening to him talk. My boss needs a wastepaper basket that occasionally says yes or no. I don't even do his letters: he's got female secretaries for those. When he's in the mood, he tells me about his wheelings and dealings, what he can get out of people by giving them a lot of credit or no credit at all, why his paper supports a certain politician, or why it prints the headlines to the local news in italics. I'm really there only because he needs someone to talk to. I'm good company."

"Is he a bachelor?"

"No, he's got a wife and two daughters, but I haven't met his family. I believe both the daughters are engaged."

"Then what does he do it for?"

"Earning money has become a sort of sport with him. He's got far more than he needs. When he has fixed up a new deal and knows what he will get out of it, or what the effect of his support will be, he allows himself the luxury of thinking. My job is to tell him about everything I've done. How I sold washing machines, for instance, or worked in a factory, or those few months I did as a sleeping-car attendant. He's always questioning me about the time when I was selling used cars, wanting to know the tricks of the trade—all about doctored engines, customers who talk like experts but don't know anything, all the things that you may or may not tell a customer. He's interested in what sort of people buy Opels or Volkswagens or foreign cars. And afterwards he makes comparisons—between car and washing-machine customers, for example."

"So, he wants to know what goes on in the big world outside, since he's sitting in the office all day long."

"No, he knows exactly what goes on."

"Maybe he's thinking of starting an advertising agency, then."

"You mean, because he sorts people into types? No, it's not that. He knows his way around there too—he uses a lot of psychological expressions. No, he's trying to apply business principles to people—the way a deal shapes up, develops, and its economic repercussions. You've got to learn to apply your own particular expertise to ordinary daily life, he says, otherwise there's no point in having it."

She whistled through her teeth. "He sounds like a foxy type. He's rich, and he thinks. That's not really your line."

"Exactly. I'm learning, and I get paid for it. Who knows how long it will last? Anyway, it's the nicest job I can think of."

When I look at it now, it does seem to me extraordinary.

But why shouldn't things go right for me once in a while? My boss is not really interested in me, he simply uses me as a sounding board that now and again speaks on its own. And because I'm young I do speak up, either against or enthusiastically for his ideas. Probably he needs to talk about his experiences before he can define and assess them properly. And anyway he has far too much humor to be satisfied just with statistics.

"Listen," I said, "he sums it all up in a sentence."

I felt she was no longer giving me her whole attention. And sure enough she asked me, "What do you get for sitting around doing nothing?"

"Eight hundred net. I've got an apartment of my own now."

"That's more than we ever had," she said.

"Why don't you listen? He says the important thing is always to achieve the satisfaction of the logical conclusion."

"And when are you going to buy yourself a car? That's something we always wanted."

"If you set up a plan, no matter what you are—a watchmaker, a worker, it's all the same—you get more satisfaction out of an achievement you planned for than when it just comes to you out of the blue. So the important thing is not only to know what you're doing, but also maybe to know what will result from it. That's of vital importance, my boss says, for achieving happiness or not."

"Your boss is a pompous ass. I suppose he has to buy himself an audience because nobody pays any attention to him at home. One thing is clear, anyway: you haven't the slightest chance of making a career for yourself in that job."

"When he's talked himself dry, he'll throw me out. But I don't care. I'll have earned some money, and I'll get a good reference."

"A pity," she said. "A real pity."

She prodded one of the kittens with the toe of her shoe. But she was careless and pressed too hard, so that the kitten let out a squeal. She took no notice, but pulled hard on her lower lip.

That gave her a tragic look. Only when the kitten clawed at her stocking did she stop and push it away.

"Now you've got the qualities which make you interesting to a woman. Don't misunderstand me. I'm talking only in general terms. Young men are charming, attractive, easy to influence. By all means let them think they're doing the leading—that's simply a matter of words. But basically they're a bore."

"Like me."

"To some extent," she said. "You put me on a pedestal, and I didn't like it up there. You tried to persuade me I was an independent-minded woman with the intelligence of a man, but that's not what I wanted to be."

"I can never understand," I felt impelled to say once more, "why women don't take their chances. They're always crying out for independence, but they never begin to fight for it, though it would be easy enough for them to undermine the world of men. In Russia there are more female than male doctors. Women become captains of ships, managing directors—"

"What do I care about Russia? You were always going on about that, when what you should have been doing was getting me with child and making us a home. But no, you despised money. You had other ideas. And what happened? What always happens in every magazine story you read: this man Luckland comes along with his horse's face and ridiculous name, invites me out, takes me around in his car, tells me what he wants and what I want, and that was exactly what I needed."

"So all right—and he paid for the divorce in the bargain. And why didn't he marry you?"

"Because I didn't want it, because all he ever did really was to send his chauffeur to get me. That wasn't enough for me. Things aren't quite as simple as that. He was the exact opposite of you, that was his charm. But was that enough? No. The way I want it is somewhere in the middle. The man must always do somewhat more than the women. After all, that's why she cooks his breakfast for him. You talked and talked about being commonsensical and the division of work between us. But women have been making the breakfast for the past five thousand years.

"Why won't you accept the fact? It's simply not true that our present age calls for a completely new way of living together. That's an invention of the Sunday newspaper supplements. All it is, is that we just have less room to move about in than before. And one day even that problem will be solved, if it must be, with all the professional know-how you men have assembled.

"A woman has less imagination than a man, and that's why she can even enjoy routine, the daily round, housekeeping, children.

"Your biggest mistake was that you always wanted to get the breakfast, in order to spare me, and you made me feel as if I was your roommate. But I was your wife, and I didn't want to feel that only in bed."

"And so now you are living with your fat friend Luise."

"I'm having a thin time at the moment, working only part-time as a switchboard girl."

"You could take an office job."

"I'm no good as a secretary, but I'm good at the switchboard."

"And that's why you're thinking about me?"

"No, you've got no proper job either. Your audience job is only another excuse for dodging the issue of growing up."

And she added, "You've got heavier."

"That's because of the eight hundred and the apartment," I said. "I've gained fifteen pounds."

"That would be the only reason for going to bed with you again."

She left me standing there and went back into the house.

At that moment I realized that my wife is a woman. I don't mean that I felt any regrets or any pity for myself. I know how she is. She gets carried away by her own intuitions, but is too lazy to do anything about them. Still, when she weeps, she weeps, and when she laughs, she laughs, until all around her feel at ease and laugh too—and then she really does begin to laugh. I admire her for that. What she does, she does whole-heartedly.

True enough, I still belong to this man with his newspaper and savings bank. I even earn a thousand marks now, but I work too. I've learned how to draw up contracts, how to evaluate people, and to have everything handy that he wants at a particular moment. But I can't say I enjoy any more of his trust on account of it. On the contrary, I'm now just one of his employees—a little cog that is allowed to perform its function. He's had people like that around him his whole life through. He has stopped telling me things, has hardly any interest in me at all. As the next step I shall probably become a departmental head in his bank or an editor on his newspaper. And then I suppose I shall really have grown up.

At supper Luise's father was back with us. In the meantime he had had a tooth pulled. It had been festering for days, but all the same he had come to the funeral.

We had cold meat, cheese, smoked fish, and pickled gherkins. With it we drank beer. The only difference from an ordinary supper was that we were all wearing dark clothes, except for little Isolde, who had on a green pullover. There was very little conversation.

Luise's father observed that the weather should stay fine to-morrow. He had a good mind to drive out to the lake. His daughter agreed, but said she couldn't go with him, as the cashier in her grill was off sick. Little Isolde offered to help out, but Luise didn't take her up on it. Kurt kept on eating steadily and a lot. He looked sad, and at times his eyes grew moist. At the start he used his knife and fork, but later he helped himself with his fingers, the nails of which were broken and full of oil. Little Isolde stared at him and then took some more meat from the dish, just because it cost her a visible effort to do so. She tries to be like ordinary people because, as she says, she has been too well brought up.

My wife ate very little. Instead, she kept plucking at her

lower lip. Every time I looked at her she gave a fleeting smile. She was no doubt thinking of her mother, or thinking she was thinking of her mother or ought to be thinking of her mother. She has a wide choice of emotional shades. I call it self-indulgence, she self-control, for she is afraid of sentimentality. I can't see that it matters, myself. After all, every emotion becomes valid as soon as one yields to it. Everything else is an academic distinction, which may provide labels for the various shades, but doesn't add to their force.

After supper we kept on drinking beer. There was also Steinhäger and a very good smooth kirsch. Luise's father was the only one to stick to vermouth on account of his sore gums.

"That was a riotous funeral," my wife said. "My mother would have enjoyed it."

"Be quiet," said Luise. "It's not a thing to joke about."

Kurt looked angry. His black hair was falling apart in the middle, and his eyes were beery.

"It was a disgrace, a thorough disgrace. There's nowhere I can show my face any more. That bitch should wash her own dirty linen first. She wants to ruin my memories of Klara. But she's wasting her time. I shall never forget Klara. Never. She'll have the finest tombstone there is, even if I have to work three years for it."

"Five," said little Isolde.

"We believe you, Kurt," Luise said. "The main thing is, she's intact in your heart."

"Klara knows that."

"And what has your wife got to say about it?" my wife asked. Kurt stared at the meat platter and said nothing. She took a piece of salami and chewed it, with a gherkin after.

"Cheers," I said.

"Don't be an idiot," said little Isolde. I was already slightly drunk.

"It's clear as daylight. She'll be glad my mother-in-law is dead. Now she and his child are in the majority."

If Kurt had not also been rather drunk he would certainly not have missed me. As it was, he slumped over the table, send-

ing the cheese flying with his sleeve, while I jumped up, pushing the television set aside behind me.

"We're not in a pigsty here," said Luise's father. We sat
down again at once as if nothing had happened. But Luise's
father got up and pointed to his cheek. His daughter tried to
keep him there with the offer of a camomile poultice, but he
shook his head and went out. After that, everyone began to
drink in earnest, and we were soon behaving more drunkenly
than we probably were. I winked at little Isolde, but she was
whispering with my wife. They were discussing some funny
business which I could not follow. There was something about
a bowling alley and red-haired Helen, who was unhappy, and
Richard with the harelip who wasn't setting up the pins any
more. I believe they sometimes hang about the pubs, softening
some man up and then leaving him flat. They are each of them
out for a bit of revenge, one because she was unlucky and the
other because she can't get what she wants.

Luise was giving Kurt some advice. He must begin now to
think of his wife, she said. He had had his way with her and
she had borne him a child, and he must take the consequences.
And anyway she loved him. Kurt would not accept that. He
had done the right thing and married her, he said, but he loved
Klara, who was now dead, and he would love Klara forever.
Luise pointed out that he must go on living and had a man's
needs. He could always remember Klara, the dead must always
be honored, but that didn't mean he should forget the living.
If he now did his duty by his family and by his work, everything would be all right. From that they went on to details.
Could he make a path for her in the garden? Kurt knew a
man who sold slate cheap. That wasn't necessary, she had already ordered some sandstone paving. Okay, he would be glad
to do it. When? Next weekend. And what if it rained?

I wandered about the room, examining the things in it.
There was a sliding door leading to another room, and I went
through. It looked just the same, except that there was a piano
standing in the corner.

Ever since my schooldays I have been able to play a foxtrot

which, when I've had something to drink, I play particularly well. I tried it, and it came to me at once. The second time through I used the sustaining pedal.

"If only I had my accordion now," said Kurt behind me.

"Just a moment."

Luise went to a cupboard and pulled out a black case. Inside it lay an accordion.

"Here's mine."

Kurt began to play. Since I knew only that one foxtrot, he tried to play along with me, but I couldn't get into his key, and stopped. We urged him to go on alone.

We continued drinking while he played, and soon we were all singing. First folk songs, and then a drinking song about the Rhine. Kurt had to stop in the middle of that, because his eyes were full of tears. He had once sung it on a pleasure boat when he was on holiday with Klara in the Rhineland. Finally we got on to ballads and the Volga Boat Song.

At some point I asked my wife to show me the washroom. Outside, she asked me to lend her twenty marks. She wanted to get away, she said. She didn't want to sleep here tonight.

"I'm not angry," she said. "And it does make things easier for Kurt. But I feel tonight I must be alone."

I had only fifteen marks.

"Is that really all you have? The cheapest hotel costs twelve marks. And I shall need a taxi."

It was really all I had.

"Well, in that case I shall just have to stay. I suppose I can put up with that on top of the rest."

"I know how it is," I said. "When you're not alone you can't have such a good guilty conscience."

"Aren't you happy at any rate that at last I have one at all?"

I went back into the room, where little Isolde was playing a march on the piano.

We didn't keep it up much longer and didn't get too loud either. When Kurt began to cry again, Luise helped him out of his jacket and tucked him up on the sofa. She told me to go up to the top of the second staircase. The maid's bedroom was free, as the maid had her day off and wouldn't be back till to-morrow.

I didn't go right up to the top at once, but into little Isolde's room on the first floor. It was a long time before she came. I heard my wife weeping next door. I also heard Luise's voice. I was waked up again by the sound of music on the radio. Little Isolde was standing in the room.

"I'm drunk," she said.

"Then you don't need to feel ashamed."

She turned off the light.

"Not so hard," she said. "Remember, we're all only women here. Oh, how I love you."

A Morning in Milan

Gerhard was just starting to make the bed when the telephone rang. The landlady came along to say that Carlo wanted to speak to him. He was surprised, for it was only an hour since Karl had gone out. He dropped the sheets and went quickly to the telephone, which was on the landing. He heard a click in the earpiece and then Karl's voice.

"Take the rest of the money and get on a streetcar to the factory. I forgot to bring my dictionary. You'd better hurry: the boss won't be gone for long. But first put on your light gray trousers, the green jacket and white shirt. If you're seen in the office, I suppose I shall have to introduce you." Gerhard passed an impatient hand over his hair, which he kept short to make him look younger. Karl was over thirty too, but you could see it.

"How long will it take you?"

"About an hour."

There was a humming noise in the telephone, then Karl's voice came through again. "Put a shine on your shoes and take my check tie. And don't forget the collar tabs. Understand?"

"Yes, of course." Gerhard fingered his neck. "I'll come at once."

He hung up, though Karl had begun to speak again. He would have to get a move on.

Back in the room, he emptied the ashtray into the waste-paper basket and threw the bedclothes into a drawer. He spread the mattress over both chairs to air. It looked tidy enough—the landlady was a demon for order. They had been glad at last to find a room on which they did not have to pay in advance. For two weeks they had been sleeping on benches in the park or in one of the three church-owned hostels. They were too old for the youth hostel, and anyway Karl didn't like the way they were run. Then Karl had got this job as a translator in a factory, though he had no work permit for Milan. That had been a real piece of luck. It wasn't going to be easy to keep going until he got his first wages, but somehow they would manage. A proper room had been the main thing.

Karl would certainly try to get to know some men from whom he could borrow money. There was no great difficulty about that in any country. This was the fourth time they had made a new start.

Gerhard would much rather have stayed on in Frankfurt, but he had met everybody there who was to be met and knew how things mostly ended: childish jealousy and backbiting, for hardly any of them really knew what they were after. Karl was mistrustful maybe, but at least he had initiative. And whenever they had any money, they had stayed indoors in the apartment, and he could feel safe. He would always be grateful to Karl for that.

Karl had been married once, to a girl in her early twenties. She had told him there was a baby on the way. It had been a real blow for Karl. In fact, the girl had only been trading on his decent upbringing. Karl married her, but no baby came. That didn't provide grounds for a divorce, Karl had said. But then the girl had the nerve to demand that Karl should give up his men friends. Karl had got into a rage and told her straight out she was jealous of his friends because he could talk to them and not to her. They were his equals, and that was something a woman could never be. Well, maybe one can get along with a woman all right, but when things get difficult they come up with all sorts of demands. And Karl had no intention of putting up with that.

Gerhard changed quickly. He had to use a belt with the light gray trousers, for they slid down over his pelvis, although he was so slim and the trousers were made to measure. Standing in his shoes, he could feel the darns in his socks digging into his heels. He could never learn to darn properly—he just pulled the holes together in a lump. The tie looked all right, the brown stain hidden away on the inside of the knot. Telling the landlady he would be back soon, he went out.

It took him a quarter of an hour to walk to the streetcar stop. He had to cross the huge Parco Sforzesco, where children were playing on the paths and old-age pensioners were sunning themselves on benches. All the pensioners here were thin. He could no longer be bothered to envy them, though he walked here often as he tried to think how he could earn some money too. It was not right to leave everything to Karl. The usual casual jobs—dishwashing, storekeeping, bricklaying—were out of the question. He simply hadn't the strength, and besides they were all sure to be taken—there was still a lot of unemployment in the town. And the offices took only women. It was different with Karl: he spoke French and English almost fluently, though his Italian was not so good.

Gerhard got on the streetcar. The journey to the outskirts cost double the usual fare. He found an empty seat and sat down, hoping there wouldn't be an influx of those bustling little women who were always about in the mornings with their bulging shopping bags.

It was all so simple really, if people would only treat you with understanding and respect. But nobody seemed able to do that. If you sweated to propagate yourself, then of course they thought the world of you and all the mess that went with it. In Japan abortions were legal and carried out free of charge.

He just couldn't see how he could have kept going without Karl, and least of all here. He had never been one of that lot who go around making eyes at everyone they meet. Companionship was important, and the feeling for it too. In practice that meant living together. Lots of famous men had done it, but he didn't see that as an excuse. Feelings don't discriminate when they are genuine and deep. And besides, there was the question of money.

The streetcar pulled into a siding to wait for another one coming toward them. Gerhard got up and went out on the open platform in front. There was not a breath of wind. His collar felt sticky, and he could feel sweat collecting in his armpits. His trousers were a bit tight in the crotch. He fingered his tie to see if it was straight. The stupid dictionary made a bulge in his jacket. He took it out of the pocket and kept it in his hand.

The streetcar moved off again. Gerhard leaned over the rail and watched the cars and motor scooters hooting as they tried to pass. The road got straight again, and the factories began. Everywhere there were great billboards covered with slogans that looked political. Settle here and you would never get out again. The high walls, the workshops with grimy glass roofs, the chimney stacks, the rail tracks with dry tufts of grass between the ties—they seemed to suck you in. Gerhard felt that without Karl he would succumb in helpless horror. Karl had once said that to work in a factory showed a criminal lack of imagination. But perhaps one could stand it for a little while here, where the language was unfamiliar and everything strange and slightly intriguing.

Gerhard caught sight of the word "Brill" on a gigantic yellow wall and got off at the next stop. The conductor had forgotten to tell him. He walked back to the factory and down a side street, and asked for Karl at the gatekeeper's lodge. A man came to show him the way. They climbed stairs and crossed corridors.

Karl was sitting alone in a little room with the door open. After the dark overalls of all the other people Gerhard had seen, the sight of Karl's white shirt was reassuring. With his glasses, his thin nose, and his tanned face Karl looked the conscientious employee, but at the same time sporting.

Gerhard did not dare enter the room. He stopped at the door and held out the dictionary. Karl rose from the desk and came out to him. "Now you've seen where I work," he said. "You'd better be off at once, before the boss gets back."

He brushed a hand over Gerhard's forehead. "You're all wet."

"It's the tie and the heavy jacket," Gerhard explained. "I'll go at once."

"Wait a moment."

Karl went back into the room and opened the drawer of his desk. "Would you like some peppermints?" he said. "You need something to suck in this heat. Have you got enough for the fare? Get some bread. There should be some cheese left. Tonight I'm going to ask for a small advance—maybe from the boss privately—and then I can bring home something to cook. I'm tired of all that cold stuff. Fill in the afternoon—go for a walk or something. Maybe you can find some detergent in the drawer—there should still be some left there. I've got no more clean shirts. Yes, and we need some sugar too."

Gerhard nodded and put a peppermint in his mouth. He watched Karl as he sat down again and looked at the papers in front of him. It would be wonderful, he thought, if one day he could work for Karl too, do things for him and protect him.

"You'd better go now," Karl said.

When Gerhard was outside he looked up at the factory wall to see if Karl was at a window. But maybe his office was on the other side. At any rate he knew now where Karl worked.

Some youths with black manes of hair were standing at the streetcar stop. They were smaller than Gerhard and had restless eyes. With types like that he never knew where he was— better keep clear of them.

An old woman was talking to the youths. They were laughing and pulling faces and pointing in his direction. The woman came over to him and said something he did not understand. The youths started to laugh again.

Gerhard went quickly into the café behind the streetcar shelter and ordered an espresso. There was a man in there, sitting at a marble-topped table eating tomatoes and bread. The girl who had served him was leaning up against the counter in an open-topped glass cubicle, fumbling in the till. Otherwise the place was empty. The long blades of an electric fan revolved slowly on the ceiling.

Gerhard heard the streetcar coming. He drank up his coffee, paid, and went out. As the streetcar drew up he glanced back at the youths, who waved to him and shouted. He looked across at the factory, read the word "Brill," and studied the brightly colored man's figure on the huge wall and the rays spreading out from his highly polished shoes.

Gerhard took off his jacket and tie and unbuttoned his shirt. The cuffs were already grimy at the edges. He decided to wash it out as soon as he got home, so as to have it ready if he was called for an interview anywhere. He had been silly to drink that espresso. Now he had only two five-lire notes left and couldn't buy himself anything—not even a roll. But there was some tobacco on the table at home with which he could roll himself a cigarette. Matches he could get from the landlady's kitchen.

Pray God Karl would not get tired of him. Why should he keep him, after all? Friendships in such complicated circumstances were not the same as marriage, and with that girl of his Karl had refused to put up with similar difficulties.

Should he follow Karl's example and try to get acquainted with some men? He had no idea whether Karl had any success on his nightly rounds, whom he met and who lent him money, and for Gerhard it would in any case be more difficult, since he spoke hardly any Italian.

He had once, quite by chance, caught sight of Karl riding in a limousine. That was before Karl got his job. It had been near the National Bank, where he liked to stand because the traffic was thickest, and in the distance he could see the cathedral through two street openings. Karl had never said whom he had been with in that car, had only mentioned vaguely that he had been out somewhere too.

Perhaps it was someone from the consulate or from the German Chamber of Commerce, where Karl had often been to make inquiries before he got his job. Yes, that was it—he remembered the license plate. No, he was wrong, it had been an English license plate. Karl knew a commercial attaché at the British consulate who had given him two suits of Scottish tweed, heavy rough stuff which could be worn here only in winter. This man had also given Karl all his shoes, but they had been too big both for Karl and for himself. The suits could of course be altered. The attaché had been transferred to Canada and would be leaving soon, Karl had said. When he went, he left his complete wardrobe behind. On the other hand Karl had also said the attaché's girl friend had got most of the suits for her brother. There had certainly been a girl in it somewhere.

Gerhard got off the streetcar at the last stop and went into the park. On the shaded paths beneath the trees women were now strolling with their children. He stopped at a pavilion.

Some people were sitting there on swinging benches piled with cushions. Swaying gently to and fro, their backs to the park, they were watching a television set which stood on a tall metal stand inside the glassed-in bar. A waiter dressed in black was serving them with cups and slices of cake. On the screen a woman in an elegant, efficiently arranged kitchen was demonstrating cooking recipes. The effortlessness and dexterity with which she worked pleased him. It did not even make him feel hungry.

The landlady opened the front door before he could insert the key. She had been snooping again. She asked him to help her move a chest of drawers, which she wanted to put in their room in place of the little dressing table with flounces. The chest was a huge and hideous thing on casters. They maneuvered it through the two-winged door. The adjustable mirror took up the whole wall between the two windows. The landlady covered the mottled imitation marble top with a worn-out oilcloth patterned with blue roses. They were paying less than the usual rent for the room, so Gerhard did not dare protest, though he knew Karl would reproach him. He would say that Gerhard should not have accepted it just so the three electricians living at the other end of the corridor could have space in their room for their bicycles.

He tried covering the fake marble top with a colored scarf,

but it was too small and looked even more ridiculous than the oilcloth.

He sat down and rolled himself a cigarette. Down in the kitchen he could hear the landlady's daughter shouting, scolding her mother and laughing shrilly. The daughter was a pushing, peroxided piece who did nothing all day except sniff around the house and wait for a man to turn up. Not long ago she had told Karl she thought it funny that the two Germans slept together in one bed. It was different, she said, for poor Italians. To judge from his tone, Karl's reply had been sharp, and she had gone back to her room without another word. The girl to whom Karl had been married must have been exactly like that, only not so blonde. How preposterous it all was!

Gerhard decided to go along to the post office afterwards. There might be a letter from one of those shifty types in Frankfurt. They would never venture into a foreign town unless they knew there was somebody there who could find his way around. Maybe somebody had sent some money. It could even be his own mother, though she knew nothing of what he was doing. She lived in her village and got picture postcards from him regularly which she could show to the neighbors. Anyway, he would walk around a bit, taking in the railway station, the American Express, and the Galleria Vittorio Emanuele Secondo, where the expensive shops were. He might try to pick up some tourists to conduct around the town or the cathedral, though they probably knew more about both than he did.

The landlady called up to him. Would he go and fetch her some bread? She kept on repeating the word "bread" as if he didn't know it. She was tired, and the stairs were bad for her heart. Her daughter would no doubt be skulking in her room and had no time because she had to think of a husband. God knows what she was really up to.

Okay, he was coming. Maybe he would get a plate of soup as a reward. He felt envious of Karl, sitting out there in his office writing letters to all corners of the earth.

Gerhard rose and put the ashtray on the bedside table.

Everything was clean and tidy. He glanced in the huge mirror above the chest. Light coming through the slits in the window blinds fell across his face. He was still nice-looking, and—more important—he looked young. But Karl never told him things like that.

The Dwelling Place

When I looked out of the window and felt behind me the room in which I had left everything as my mother had arranged it— the table, the ceiling lamp, the sideboard, the sofa, the piano, the easy chair, and the iron stove that heats so well and in which I could put my hot-water bottle to warm all day, to bub-ble and sing in my dear little stove that heats so well—when I felt all that, looking out of my attic window and surveying our dear little town with the three church spires and the two old gates which had survived all fires in medieval times, in the Thirty Years' War and during the Napoleonic occupation, then I knew that I ought to be happy here. You can always come down and play with him, she had said.

It is summer, the meadows full of gold. Even Solomon in all his glory was not arrayed like one of these. I must do some practice. Every day down in the yard below my mother used to split kindling for the fire out of the waste from the sawmills. She would sit in her black dress on the stool and use the big kitchen knife to split the sticks from top to bottom. She had lost everything. One hundred thousand gold marks she had planned to leave her children, she had got up at four o'clock in the morning, walked a full hour to our dairy, had checked on everything and given orders, had walked back again and then worked the whole day through, serving guests in our inn. And then in the inflation everything was gone. We sold the little brewery and the inn and had kept only the house. The lower floor we had let, and she had remained cheerful till the day of her death. Toward the end she had hardly been able to move her fingers, the joints had become so stiff. I'm getting like that myself now. I must do some practice. The vicar gets impatient if I play the hymns too slowly.

They were a brave young couple. I saw right away that things were a strain on her, for she was rather delicate. The baby, a little boy, was like neither of them. It had large eyes, but no hair yet. It was not an easy child, it could get impatient and yell, but she did her best, one must admit that. He was a vet, just starting his practice. There are already three vets in the town, but he was determined to establish himself. He was a hard-working young man, and he always greeted me politely. If he had spoken our local dialect he would have found more clients. Country folk are cautious.

I must do some practice. The vicar is usually late in putting the list of what he wants on Sunday in my letter box. He is always short of time. When he gets out of his car he leaves the motor running. He is such a cheerful man. I enjoy it, he says, I am happy and thankful, I praise the Lord when I see a schnitzel on the platter before me, bacon and a bottle of beer, when the stopper pops and the beer flows down to my stomach. Why should I not enjoy what the good Lord grants? And of course he is right.

His wife is a solid person too. She is an orthopedic surgeon, and she spends nearly every day in Fachlings, where there is a convalescent home that belongs to an insurance company. She helps the doctor there to treat slipped disks. She makes a tidy sum, he told me once, laughing. I laughed too, for I know he earns well over a thousand marks a month himself. They neither of them can keep things neat, but that doesn't worry them. The three children are looked after by old Lampacher, who had worked for years at the Lutheran hospital. He does the shopping and the cooking, cleans the rooms and does the laundry. My wife loves her job, he says, and the children love old Lampacher, who considers himself indispensable, so why should I worry? I don't mind at all what people say, though I am the vicar. Yes, I must say this for him, he is a good vicar, even if he is a little on the loud side. And she is said to be a good doctor: people certainly like her. All the same, I wish he would put the song list for Sundays in my letter box by Thursday at the latest. I cannot play by heart, I've got to read from the score, but that has to be practiced too.

For twenty-seven years I played in the Georgskirche, but now I play only in the country districts: in the Meierhöfen village school; in the chapel of the Überruh sanatorium, where a Protestant service is held once a month; in the Ratzenried community center; in the new gym at Herlatz; and in Biesbach, Rötensteig, Toblach, and Seufzgen. Most of these places have a harmonium, two have a piano, and only the Überruh chapel has a small organ. I used to enjoy playing in the Georgskirche, but young Fräulein Reischer has had proper training, whereas I am entirely self-taught. In praising God it's not ability that counts, the vicar once told me.

Every other Sunday we travel about, summer and winter. And invariably he is late. He rings the doorbell and then immediately starts blowing his horn. But I have two flights of stairs to come down, and I like to take a quick peep at the baby, which may just then be being fed. The young couple would be sitting before the Son. My brother could have been living there now. He too could have a dear wife and a son, and celebrate Sunday mornings in the family circle. But he is dead, and I am the only one left.

Why must he always hoot like that? I'm not far short of sixty. I'm hurrying. I've still got the use of my legs. He's younger, and he doesn't need to blow his horn. I must make sure I have everything: the list of hymns, the music, the prayer book. The last time, he forgot his gloves in my music case. His hands sweat on the steering wheel.

In the first car he had everything used to rattle, and in winter he often got stuck. We had to dig ourselves out, and I would put my coat over the hood, so that the engine would start again. Once we had to get some horses to pull us out of a ditch. We can't have an accident until after vespers, he said with a laugh. The prospect of a hearty supper after Evensong makes him happy, that I know. He has a secondhand Mercedes now, which his wife is said to have paid for. So far he has had no trouble with it, except for a single blowout. He was so impatient that I had to turn the screws on the hubs myself. We arrived late, and he began the sermon directly after the first hymn. However, in country districts people have an understanding for things like that. The meek shall blossom forth and multiply. I am thankful for my humble heritage.

He also gives lantern-slide lectures for the patients at the convalescent home in Fachlings. He buys everything on installments: his tape recorder, his camera, his tent, his projector. His evening gatherings are very popular. He has been everywhere on his holidays with his wife and children and old Lampacher. To Lake Constance, of course—that's not so very far away—but also to Carinthia, to Yugoslavia, and to the French and Italian seacoasts. I often wonder how the family manage in their tent, cooking and sleeping all together. She is an excellent doctor, but how old Lampacher keeps house in a tent, that really defies imagination. The vicar takes excellent photographs. And now he has a faltboat as well.

He has already given two lectures for the Württemberg Bible Society, one in Schwäbisch Gmünd and one in Bad Wurzach. He is really very knowledgeable. Sometimes during the sermon —I always know when—he loses his concentration and cuts it short, because he is hungry. Being a clergyman is the best occupation in the world, he says, I can think of nothing better, but I've got to eat. He who mortifies himself is suspect.

I hurried down the stairs, hearing the baby's crowing as I passed, and then I was seated in the car, and off we went. He was quite red in the face. Once a year he goes to the municipal hospital for a general checkup. Physically he is very strong, and every spring he digs his large garden by himself. I have to watch myself, since I have trouble with my digestion. Often I cannot sleep and I get hot flushes and palpitations because nothing passes through. I drink two cups of digestive tea every evening, but it no longer has much effect. Perhaps, since my digestive system is already letting me down, I may die of cancer. Without raw salads I should be lost.

He has a collection of colored maps on which every path,

every stream, and even the smallest rise is indicated. Once recently he took his faltboat with him, and after the sermon we drove out to the Blaichensee, which is out on the moors. He put the faltboat together, and we had to search the heather for two wing nuts. He was angry, for he had intended to show me how quickly he could get the boat assembled. The joints on the planks got stuck too. Vicar, I told him, if you don't take things more easily you'll be having a heart attack. Get in, he said, laughing, get in! The Lord is my shepherd, I shall not want. He leadeth me to a canoe and biddeth it to shoot across the waters. He commandeth the beasts of the field and offereth me frogs on the leaves of water lilies. That is his way: he turns everything to his own amusement and advantage. His wife is lucky to have him. The faltboat all but turned over before he finally got settled in it.

Pleasure is rare. That I have cause to know since my mother lost everything in the inflation and had to work her fingers to the bone to bring me and my brother up. I serve my church as an organist. In earlier days I could play quite well, but my legs are short, and it is difficult to reach the pedals. But I am thankful I can still be of use somewhere in the parish. The seed springs up everywhere.

We paddled across the Blaichensee. At first I couldn't keep time with him and my arms ached, but the vicar kept going until we were in the rushes. There we lay still a long time, waiting. At last, when the sun was already setting, the tufted ducks and moorhens came out. He took four color pictures before they noticed us and dived out of sight.

Have you brought a bathing suit? he asked me. Do you mind if I have a swim? Vicar, I replied, you can swim when you are with your family. If anyone should see us, you would be laughed at. A vicar must set the example.

In America the clergymen have airplanes, he said. I was really angry then. There are many different sects in America, I said. That is their affair. You are a Protestant preacher, and you have a family. In America, he said, there are automatic organs which are played by electricity. In America, I said, and began to paddle again, in America everything is different. Here, you cannot impress people by not being an old-fashioned parson. You have no need to advertise. You have nothing to sell. You must be like everybody else. Nobody here has an airplane.

That will come, he said. Perhaps I shall buy a trailer. The tent is too small for the whole family. But basically you are quite right. We paddled together back to the car.

He is a good vicar, even if he gives lectures and spends all his money on photography and plays symphonies on his tape recorder to the patients at the convalescent home. If he were to become the number-one local minister, he would have more responsibility, and no more time for his hobbies. The fact that his wife earns money also encourages him in his ways. I don't say that in her place I should pay more attention to the children: after all, she is an orthopedic surgeon with a long training behind her.

In my attic I would sit sewing for the refugees. I knitted pullovers, I cut out aprons, I thought out clothes which were practical and could be made at home on a sewing machine. At Christmastime I had ten whole parcels complete. I looked out over the roofs of the town and thought of the families living under them: large and small families, prospering or breaking up—the vicar's family, the young vet's downstairs in my own house, the photographer's, the butcher's, the hairdresser's, the mayor's. They all grow larger or smaller, they have their joys and their sorrows, their hopes and anxieties. They sit together at table and eat, they laugh and get cross, they lie in bed and pray, they turn out the light and whisper, they run temperatures and have bread poultices put on them, they have to get up early in the morning and fill thermos bottles for the menfolk, send the children off to school, fill up two baskets in a morning's shopping, count their money and watch what they spend. They flourish and separate, but are still one flesh and blood. There were times when I needed to play a lot of hymns on the piano to find the will to go on.

They called him Kicker, Lablab, or Monkey Face. I could hear his little tantrums through the glass door when I went down to the cellar to fetch the milk or potatoes. They were a nice young couple with a sweet little boy. You can play with him whenever you like, she said.

She was pressing cottage cheese through a sieve, mashing slices of banana with a fork, adding a little orange juice, everything well mixed and whipped to a froth. This is what he likes best of all, she told me. She sweetened the mash with plenty of sugar. I was allowed to taste it.

He had the front room to himself, the one that had been our best room, where we had drunk cocoa on Sundays when my mother was still alive and my brother came home for the holidays. The walls are now covered with a bright paper. There is a table with a gay check oilcloth for changing diapers, a cupboard, a chest of drawers, and a cot. During the daytime he would be in his playpen, but he could not yet pull himself upright on the bars. She put him in the high chair and tied a bib around his neck.

When I sat down on a chair beside them he did not cry at all, just made a face. I put the little wooden cart I had bought on the tray in front of him. Look, this is your new auntie, who is going to see that our little man eats properly and fills himself up. You mustn't talk now, she said, or he won't eat.

She brought the little bone spoon full of baby food up to his mouth, but he did not open it. His large head with its white skin leaned lopsided against the back of the chair. He had an anxious look. Little monkey, I said, little monkey. He pushed at my toy cart once, then pulled back his hand.

With thumb and forefinger she tweaked his cheek and forced his mouth open. He was about to yell, but the baby food was in his mouth before he could utter a sound. Bravely he swallowed it down, and then began to cry. Now he will eat, she said. I always have to force the first spoonful on him, otherwise he doesn't know what he has to do.

Each time he paused for breath she plunged the full spoon deep into his mouth so as to coax him into swallowing. He was gradually sliding further and further down in the chair, his legs dangling, and, whenever the spoon approached him, he just moved his head from side to side. He was soundlessly weeping. His face was wet and smeared with baby food. It was dreadful. He has got to eat, she said.

I don't think you should force him, I felt impelled to say. He should be cheerful, but he is crying. He must eat, she said, or he won't grow. She tried once more with a full spoon, but the food ran out of his mouth and down his neck. She wiped him vigorously with a paper napkin. Perhaps he doesn't like cottage cheese, I said. It's good for him, she said, he must eat it. She is right about that, of course. Cottage cheese is good for you. I eat it myself, mixed with caraway seeds.

While she was clearing up in the kitchen, I sat on the floor beside the playpen. He was inside it, lying on his tummy and scarcely moving. I stretched a hand through the bars and kept picking up a mug or a block and letting it fall. He watched, but did not reach out for it. In the end I had to kneel, since my back was hurting. I took up a block and let it clatter and bounce on the linoleum in front of the playpen. Curious, he crawled nearer. I repeated the movement several times, so that he should learn. Suddenly he thrust a hand through the bars and brushed it back and forth, knocking the block under the wardrobe. I lay down on the floor to retrieve it. As I went on making it bounce and clatter, he turned over on his back and stayed in that position. For quite a while I kept on picking up mugs and blocks in both hands and dropping them down in front of him.

I was still there when she sat him down on his pale blue plastic throne, which had a bulge at the back for support and a narrow projection in front to catch the little stream. He sat there as good as gold, picking at his rolled-down panties. We waited quietly. He must learn to concentrate, she said.

And indeed in a little while—the time did not seem long to me—she suddenly cried, There!—though I had noticed nothing. We both cried There encouragingly, and in the pot there lay a portion, light and dark together. Breakfast and dinner, she said, lifting him up.

While she was wiping him clean with cotton wool on the

table and creaming his lower parts, I took a good look at our little hero. His tiny arms were chubby, but otherwise he was thin, and you could see his ribs. It was just that he was slimly built. His skin had a yellowish tinge. With hair on his head he would have looked Italian. There was a pink rash across his whole tummy. That comes from the rubber pants, she said, they're far more practical than cotton diapers. He wriggled about and was happy. And of course it is an exertion, as I know.

We went on talking for a while in the living room. I suggested that she might like to take over one half of the garden, so that she could grow vegetables and kitchen herbs. Thank you, she said, it's really very kind of you, but I know absolutely nothing about gardening. Then her husband came in, and I went away. He looked pale, and there were shadows under his eyes. I suppose he often gets called out in the night when his older colleagues feel disinclined. He accompanied me to the foot of the stairs. As I was going up, I heard him swear, and inside the apartment a door slammed.

The infant child, the little onion head with no hair and too much skin, gurgling, unable as yet to speak its will, wholly dependent. The son, begotten by the father, by the mother conceived, it binds from the beginning.

The vicar was very kind and took Frau Sistig by car to the hospital in Leutkirch. I hear she is very poorly. It was only this spring that we celebrated her seventieth birthday with a little party. Her granddaughter, who is a pharmacist's assistant in Ravensburg, was there with us. People kept knocking at the door, and the occupants of neighboring rooms came to wish her many happy returns and to bring some chocolate, a bunch of flowers, or even a bottle of eggnog. She was very proud of herself for having decided to go into the old people's home. One must make room for others, she said. I can knit just as well here, and when I go to visit my daughter once a year the pleasure is all the greater. The vicar thinks she will never come out of the hospital. She has got thin and can hardly eat anything. She is beginning to go the same way as me. If I had always been given the hymn list in plenty of time, I could have practiced much more. I must keep on playing, playing and praising the Lord. Maybe I should simply make the digestive tea twice as strong, but then it overstimulates me. An alarming pressure builds up in the intestines during the night and mounts to the heart: I have to jump out of bed and walk quickly around the table a number of times. Sometimes I find a cold footbath helps.

Or should I do some sewing, or grate a radish and drink the juice? I am quite alone in the world.

In the mornings I like to lie in bed for a while. Far away, from the brewery opposite which was once ours, I can hear the rumbling of beer kegs being moved around. It reminds me of my childhood days, when I once had to spend a whole year resting on the couch because of a weak spot on the upper lobe of my lung. My mother had to run the entire place herself and, every Wednesday after the fermentation, load the malt mash on the wagon single-handed. My lung eventually healed right up. In my mind's eye I see the men filling the kegs and loading them up, hosing the ground, reckoning and telephoning, while I lie warm in bed every morning in my attic. If that is your only sin, the vicar once told me, good luck to you.

I couldn't go with him. He has his wife, his children, and his hobbies, he is a parson and in the full flower of his years. It is kind of him to find time every week to drive to Leutkirch especially to visit Frau Sistig. I shall ask him to take her a letter. Before I became an organist I was an assistant nurse at the Überruh sanatorium. The doctor who had treated me for my lung weakness got me the place. At that time it was not restricted to tubercular patients only. On several occasions I was present at operations for goiter. A specialist came from Stuttgart to do them. Long needles were stuck into the patient's throat, and the tumor was cut out under a local anesthetic. It was very instructive. Once a woman died during the operation.

Together with a young probationer I wheeled the body on a hospital trolley to the mortuary, which was windowless. We pulled back the sheets and laid her down on the tiled slab.

She was middle-aged. The large wound on her neck was a red bowl with sinews, and the white gullet bent with every movement of the head. We were inexperienced in the job. I stuffed the sheets into a bucket and closed the lid. Then we washed the body down with diluted vinegar. I had to keep squeezing out the sponge. The other nurse nearly fainted, for the excrement on the thighs smelled strongly. She had to leave the room. If I had not been able to weep, I could not have stood it either. I covered up the throat wound with a piece of wax paper and on top of that I tied a napkin. The dead woman was a farmer's wife, and I felt sure her relatives would want to get her and bury her at home. Everybody in the village would want to have a last look at her. My sacrifice was not in vain. I washed down my mother all by myself when her time came.

Chives, beets, cauliflower—she could have had some of the apples too, and the cordon pears, the currants and gooseberries. It's nothing to be ashamed of, not knowing anything about gardening. And it isn't as if I had asked her to rake over the path when his car leaves tire marks on it. She had enough to do already, what with her little duckling and having to watch the telephone all day too. Every call could mean a job for him. I wanted to leave the strip under the trees uncultivated and to make a lawn of it, so that next year the little fellow could have been playing in the grass, smelling the flowers, and listening to the buzzing bees. The young couple could have sat on a blanket and watched their son growing up strong in the sunshine. She came into the room without knocking. Please, she said, please help me.

She leaped down the stairs, I after her. She quickly showed me everything: the bottle, the milk, the oat flakes. I was to heat the milk in the bottle, then stir it with the flakes into a mash. I did not need to bathe him, for she would be back directly. She had every confidence in me. And all the time she was crying, taking money from the breadbox and putting it in her handbag. What is it? I asked. You mustn't lose your head.

I saw her, she said. They drove past together in the car.

Whenever he was called out in the night for a birth or because the pigs everywhere are infected with murrain, he has been going to her. Last night was the same. I rang up the farmer in Stiefenhofen this morning, where he was supposed to have been, and he hadn't been there at all. I'm going back to my parents, she said. I've had enough, she said, there's some orange juice still in the icebox. She went off in tears, taking an umbrella with her, though the weather was fine.

The son, the infant boy, born of suffering. I felt at my wits' end, yet I did everything exactly as she had instructed me. He sat there as good as gold in his high chair, playing with a cold cream carton which she had put on the tray in front of him. He opened his mouth obediently and let me put in a spoonful of baby food, then another and another. He would eat for me.

But afterwards I did not know what to do. I put him back into his playpen and waited. I was simply unable to bring myself to believe that the young couple had broken up. I stood up and looked down on the child. His mother, his father, it is my house in which they lived. Then the telephone rang.

I went into the hall and picked up the receiver. Is my wife not in? he said when I answered. What about the child? I explained that I was looking after it, but I did not tell him what she had said to me. Ah yes, now I remember, he exclaimed, we had arranged to meet in the market square, and now I am late. Not the market square, I said, the railway station, and you had better hurry. He swore, and hung up the receiver.

Suddenly all my apprehension vanished. Strength and gratitude welled up inside me. I had been chosen to receive the innocent Lamb!

I lifted him up, pressed him to me, and for the first time felt his body against mine. The Son lay in my arms. I hurried upstairs.

I walked around and hummed songs to lull him to sleep. When I struck a few notes on the piano, he began to cry. I put him on the sofa, where he immediately quieted down. Then I lit a fire in my stove, put water in a metal bowl, and placed it in the opening of the oven above the flames to heat, in the place where in winter I always kept my hot-water bottle. I hung two towels to warm over the back of a chair. It got quite warm in my room, and I opened the door to the kitchen. As the water was heating up, I tried to feed the child with slices of apple, but as yet he had no teeth. He began to choke, and I had to dig in his mouth with my finger to fetch out the bits. He was crying and dribbling sour mucus all over the sofa.

Once more I had to leave the Son alone as I poured the hot water into the sink and ran in cold to bring it to body temperature. Then I laid him down on the table in the kitchen, which was now also very warm, and took off his clothes: rompers, knitted shoes, shirt, panties, and the button-up rubber pants. Cautiously I bent the thin arm and leg joints, trembling with the effort not to hurt him. At last he was lying naked before me. He was not very wet! Just on the hips there was a little powder clinging still. Slowly I lowered him into the water. I had to support him under the arms, since his head kept falling to one side. He stretched his body out and moved his limbs. I sprinkled him, scooped water up in my right hand, and let it run in lukewarm rivulets over his chest and stomach. There he lay in his Jordan and was cleansed. And his little pale flower rocked to and fro in the water.

Afterwards I dried him and rubbed his whole body with surgical alcohol, as I do my own to harden it. He did not cry, but just lay there, small and pale. The bath had tired him. I dressed him again in his rubber pants and wrapped him in two pillowcases.

I was still rocking him in my arms when I heard them come in downstairs. I heard doors being slammed, then silence, and then they began to shout. The child was lying at my breast.

All of a sudden the vicar was standing in my room. How hot it is, he said, you must open the window. The child, vicar, I said, look, the child is here with me. I have bathed him, and now he is sleeping.

He did not even look at the child properly, simply said what a poor little mite it was. He laid a new list of hymns on the table. The bishop would be attending the service at the sanatorium, he said. A niece of his had just been admitted as a patient. Begin each hymn with a prelude—a fugue or something. You must start to practice now. I held the child out to him, but he was already out of the room, clumping off down the stairs. After his car was gone, they started again down below.

Swine, I could hear them shouting, skunk, I'll kill you. I stood at the top of the stairs, listening, the Son pressed tight against me. She ran into the bedroom and locked the door. He swore and shouted and rattled the handle until she opened it again. He went inside and slammed the door shut, and then there was silence. I waited a long time, leaning far over the banisters, holding the child tight and listening. But they did not come out again. I felt like laughing. I locked my door too.

My butterfly, my son! I lay there in bed, he on top of me. I took off my dress, since the room was so warm. At first he did not move, just blinked and kept opening and shutting his hand, but then he crawled out of the pillowcases up toward my chin. As soon as he reached it I pushed him down, and he made efforts to regain his position. His little fingers clung obstinately to my flesh, and his legs pushed at me as he sought to reach his goal. In his eagerness a little bubble of spit formed on his rosy mouth. I closed my eyes and let him do as he pleased.

Then I called out Hup! and Whoops! He gurgled, for I had tossed up my chest. I did it again. It went even better with my stomach. I really made him hop. As I jerked up my body again and again, he stretched out his arms and legs and let out little cries of joy. I was panting with the exertion.

At first she came alone to the door and knocked. I pressed him to me and did not move. It was very kind of you, she said, to look after him. I made no reply, and scarcely breathed. You must be hearing me, she cried, and drummed on the door with her fists. Why don't you answer? The child got restless and was about to cry out, so I had to cover it up with a pillow. Open the door, she was shouting. Then she stopped and went off down the stairs. I jumped out of bed.

In the sideboard, behind the stove, on the floor, between the sofa and the piano, where was the safest place? I saw him lying there on my bed, yelling, arms and legs stretched out. His pale hairless head was now red and swollen. I had to go to him in bed and rock him. His sobs gradually became quieter. I kissed the teardrops from his cheeks. I lay there, held him high above me and, exulting, summoned up my strength.

They came together and knocked on the door. They pleaded and shouted, threatened and offered me money, but I gave them no answer. I kept raising the pillow that lay on the Son, so that he could breathe. And in one such moment he betrayed me. But I did not make a sound myself until they broke down my door with an ax.

I put out all my strength to protect the child. When they rushed at me, I covered it with my body. They seized me and tried to turn me over, but I held fast to the bed frame with both hands. They struck me and tore at me, but it was of no avail. We were all shouting and struggling, but only I was strong, for beneath me lay the Child. The husband twisted my arm, and the pain made me lose my grip on the frame. I fell over on my side, but with the other hand I grabbed the child. He was trying to snatch it from me, but his wife pushed in front of him. Don't, she cried. When they saw the child they both gave up.

I clutched it to me and leaped from the bed. Before they could stop me I was in the kitchen, had torn open a drawer to get a fork or a knife. Then a blow from behind threw me down across the table. I do not know how they got the Son away from me and left the room.

I can hear them now downstairs, talking and telephoning. I am lying in bed, waiting and keeping in the warmth. Cast down, on the third day risen, ascended, there He sits to the right of the Father, whence He will come again to redeem us.

Fortresses must be raised about the tabernacle where the chalice stands to receive the blood. All will see the Lamb that sits at the gate, surrounded by pillars of fire, sharpened scythes and sickles, and the Revelation will come from His mouth with a voice of thunder. I see and feel the glory, when they shall smite me and devour my flesh, because I must warm and comfort. Lord, I call to Thee, I am Thy dwelling place.

A Monotonous Landscape

Since the house is my own and I like it here, I stay in the housing development. The countryside is pleasant too. The people are Lutherans, and thrifty—they like to own the houses they live in, so I sell them insurance policies against injury, death, fire, flood, and theft. My predecessor worked hard, and so do I. If you make regular rounds, keep pegging away at everybody who shows a bit of interest, you can earn enough in these country places. And as time goes on I begin to pick up a bit of the local dialect. That helps too.

I have a couch in the kitchen and a wardrobe in the hall. That is all I need. Everything else is stacked in the living room, and the two rooms upstairs are empty. That's the way I like it. I live in the kitchen, but I have the whole house to myself. Whenever I look into the living room, or go upstairs to the two empty rooms above, I feel happy. I look through the window at the other houses in the development. They stand very close together, and every window is curtained. I have curtains only in the kitchen at the back, though one of the windows looks out over a rye field and is always open anyway, unless it's raining. When I watch television, I shut the window that looks out on the street. The television set stands on a little high table at the foot of the couch, so I can watch it lying down.

I must watch my figure, that fat bitch says, that fatso wrapped around the middle in an apron, that hideous wobbling gelatin with thinning hair and sweat marks on her blouse. She of all people, that fat, loathsome slob, tells *me* I must watch my figure, when I'm tall and thin and fair-haired and brown all over from swimming in every river and pond I come across.

I didn't answer back, I just laughed and went inside the house. A flowered rolling-pin, that's what she is, with a perverse imagination. All she wants is to show off to the neighbors, standing gossiping there in front of their houses, elbows on the wire-mesh fences, yak-yakking from garden to garden, across the string beans, the primulas, the rabbit hutches and cabbage patches, every morning till the kids come home from school and every afternoon till their men come home from work. I am new in the development and have neither wife nor child. They don't know a thing about me, and that's why they gossip and let their imaginations off the leash to come sniffing around my legs. I shall give her that bicycle just the same.

No, I won't. Of all the crazy ideas—to give her a brand-new bicycle! It's a racing bicycle, a French one with narrow tires, chromium rims, blue enameled frame, and handlebars of a sort unknown in these parts. I can just see her mother scolding and nagging, pinching and poking her in the ribs, banging her between the shoulder blades. Then her father will join in too, and they'll talk a lot of nonsense until in the end she'll have to give the bicycle back to me. They'll make her push it down the road to my house, and you can bet all the neighbors will be standing at their windows watching. She'll lose her nerve, and who can blame her with all those people looking on? She won't dare to knock at my door. She'll just lean it up against the fence, my lovely, expensive bicycle which I wanted to see her ride, watch her sinewy legs pushing and pumping, her skirt billowing in the breeze. I hear her ringing the bell, then a final glimpse as she disappears around the corner at the top of the road. But no, she'll lean this splendid, gleaming thing up against the fence—I've got one of those too, though behind it I let things grow as they will—and then walk back the way she came, fighting back her tears. It makes me laugh.

I know very well what they are all thinking. Maybe I am all alone in my house, but I've got a television set. And anyway I'm off to bed early, since I often have to get up at the crack of dawn to catch all the people I have to see. They live far apart from one another. And it's seldom I get home early. They have to be talked into it, these small fry, these penny-pinchers, these cheese-paring nitwits, who all want a house of their own —oh, yes, indeed—but can't decide whether to pay it off in twenty or in thirty years. And it takes time to explain it all, to work out in detail capital investment, interest rates and mortgages—God, there are times it almost kills me.

But I get around it, I find plenty of chances when the men are at work and the women stuck in the kitchen, reading the newspaper or wondering what to cook. I tell them what's in the papers and what they should cook. They're grateful for anything that's not routine, that's new and gives them a bit of excitement. I would only have to give a wink—but I don't. I go off for a swim in the rivers and fishponds I drive past on the way, because I enjoy swimming and being by myself, while they skulk in their kitchens and living rooms, thinking of me and indulging secret thoughts, because it gives them a thrill. I know exactly what I want. I wanted to give her something— a bicycle at the very most—but she won't get it now. It makes me laugh, yet I feel sorry for her. At her age I would have done a lot for a bicycle like that.

When I was only waist-high I and my friend used to go in fine weather to the railway station. Dressed in our leather shorts and green hats, we would position ourselves on the platform, and as the train came in he would play the concertina while I yodeled. In those days our little town had a reputation as a health resort, and the holidaymakers getting off the train were touched by the sight of two kids making music to welcome them. They stopped, gave us coins, and were eager for more, but we always had to cut it short, since the train came in at noon precisely and we both had to be home for dinner on the stroke of twelve. We never earned more than a mark apiece, having to leave off at once like that on account of the midday meal. And in the end my mother and my friend's mother decided to put a stop to our musicmaking, in case anything happened to us— children did sometimes get picked up and taken off. We were annoyed at the time, but we quickly forgot about it. The money we earned would never have bought us a bicycle, and in any case there were no racing bicycles available in our town at that time. It makes me laugh again to think of it.

So here I sit in my own house in the development, ready and waiting. But it won't happen as I visualize it. They won't come—together, singly, from all sides at once—to beat on my door, break in my windows, plow up my garden, and shake their fists at me. They'll be sitting at their kitchen or living-room tables, or maybe watering those gardens of theirs which I can't see from my window—or at any rate not all of them—or they'll have gone off to the bar. They don't talk about it any more, or they've forgotten, or perhaps they never even noticed it in the first place. To hell with them.

Of course, there are a lot of children in the development, some of them pretty children with rosy cheeks and little wet noses, grimy hands and scratched knees. Whether she is particularly pretty I can't really say, but on me she has certainly made an impression. I get the shivers whenever I think of her.

She told me she'll be leaving school in half a year from now. I asked her what she wanted to be—a typist, a salesgirl, I couldn't think of anything else. She wasn't even listening. All she wanted to do was to swim, in the same river and at the exact spot I always swim when my business takes me that way. She went there on foot, walking three or four miles in the afternoon heat. It is a place where the river widens out, and there are sandbanks in the middle. There is sand too on the river banks and willow trees behind, and I always swim there in the nude, for I have never met a soul, and you can't get to it by car. You have to leave your car on the common and then walk alongside a field of rye and scramble over a couple of wooden fences, which I enjoy most of all, since all the other fences around here are wire ones, and electrified. As I drew up and got out of the car, she was just turning off from the road. She asked me right away if I was going swimming too. She had often seen me in the development, she said, I must be new. I had never seen her before. She is fourteen.

I turned back and got my swimming trunks from the car.
She laughed and said she had brought her swimming suit along
too, just in case. I was surprised—girls of her age aren't usually
so frank.

She swims very well, and so do I. Naturally I have
more strength. Doing the crawl as fast as I can, I can just get
through the whirlpool between the two sandbanks. She did not
start to undress until I had slunk off into the bushes, getting
scratched in the process. I could just see her as she went behind a bush farther down the river and kept turning around to
see if I was looking. We were alone, the road is a long way from
the river, and very few cars drive past. So I got a move on and
went straight into the water.

She is thin, her arms and legs are too long and the joints are
knobbly. Her shoulder blades, rippling about under her swimsuit, are skinny. She has long hair, and now she had tied it into
a pigtail. Her skin is burned brown—browner than mine. She
hitched up her swimsuit before getting into the water, disclos-
ing a strip of white above her thighs. Ugh, she said, it's cold.

The river, with its sandy shores against a silver wall of wil-
lows, is the loveliest river I know. The water flowing down
from the moors is dark, yet the sand is whiter than any other
I have seen. The river at this point is wide and deep, and flows
slowly but with a powerful thrust that carries everything before it. And in the middle there are these two smooth sandbanks, covered with clumps of grass nodding in the wind. Between them lies the whirlpool, which I find so tempting to
swim through, since I can only just do it. And no sooner am I
on the one sandbank than I want to be on the other, building
dams, ramming in posts and weaving twigs between them. I
want to gallop along the banks, become a beaver and gnaw,
dive down, and build up my river, block it, make a swamp of
it, so that nobody else shall have it. And now she is there too.

She has quick frog's legs and tadpole arms. As she streaks
through the water, the snaky garland of her hair bobs up and
down. I overtake her, take a mouthful of water and, turning,
spurt it in an arch over her head. Swimming upstream, I battle

against the current. Then, puffing and blowing, I wait for her, and she catches hold of my feet and lets me drag her along.

I really looked at her properly only when she was dressed again and we were walking back across the common to the road. She had on a child's dress and sandals, and as she walked, dangling her handbag, she pulled in her breast. I am pleased with myself for having noticed this involuntary action. I can well imagine that they feel ashamed when it begins to grow. I don't really know—why should I? I am neither her brother nor her father, but just a very distant neighbor. She wanted a switch, a stick with leaves only at the very top. I broke off a little willow branch and peeled it right down to the last leaf cluster. And as we walked toward the road she slashed it about, slicing a couple of leaves from a bush, flattening a tuft of grass, decapitating buttercups, rapping the wooden fence. Then she stopped to draw circles in the sand. I took the switch out of her hand and, keeping my eyes on her, swung it whistling past her head very close. I did it once, maybe twice, and felt quite sick. She laughed and shook her head as I lashed around, hearing the fine agonized note of the switch cutting through the air. I swung it above her head, touching a hair that stuck up behind, and then I gave the switch back to her. Laughing, she ran on ahead. There is a dark filling in one of her front teeth.

She had not been to the sandbanks often. She had wanted to be alone, quite alone, and so she had walked the whole way, along the road, in spite of the heat. She walked back too. She did not get into the car, though I should have been glad to drive her home. Standing beside the car, she began to withdraw into herself, blushed, became tongue-tied, and seemed suddenly less than fourteen years old, perhaps only ten—as I said, I don't know about these things. I drove on in the opposite direction and watched her in my rear-view mirror. She did not turn, but walked straight in the direction of her home.

And now she'll be sitting on the sofa in the kitchen, eating. All of the people in the development eat in the kitchen, but they don't, like me, live in it too. On the left sits her father, a great black-haired clod, a bulldozer, swilling, guzzling, shoveling down his food with goggling eyes fixed on his wife opposite. She sits to the right of her daughter, her one and only, her chick, her primrose, who will soon be leaving school and doesn't know what she wants to do later. The father doesn't give a damn, but the bloated placenta, that giant ovary fed on rich cakes and melted butter, she won't be able to slobber over her little sprat any more, to maul her and press her to her aproned belly. She will be worrying and fretting, because she too doesn't know, nor does Father, who anyway mustn't be disturbed at the sacred task of filling his belly. On wooden chairs they sit and chew, to either side of their little cushioned darling, who will run to fat herself one day, though that needn't worry me, for at present she is thin.

Of course I shall stay here in the development, where I have my own house that's paid for, even if it isn't very large, even if there is a rye field at the back and the road in front is a dirt track. But I am not one of them. This girl and I—and, since I'm much older than the girl, she will hardly even have noticed what is hatching in her mother's sparrow's brain—the two of us—and her name might be Brigitte for all I care—we two have hit on something which these fumblers, these microgiants from the development have no conception of. Maybe I am the only one who knows it. In that case the girl won't even be to blame and won't be lying in bed up in her attic thinking of me, in the way people like to pretend. It's never as bad as it's made out to be.

I am sitting in my kitchen too, I haven't turned on my television, but am thinking of them whispering, sniggering, picking their ears and examining their fingers in an effort to squeeze ideas from their sluggish brains. I don't give a damn where my house stands or what it is made of—brick, wood, or concrete. I have this one in the development, and then only because I work for the company. But I am free, and I can go swimming with this girl, and I know—I knew it for sure when I saw her walk off down the road—that she won't tell a soul. The development has no idea.

She walked the three or four miles, on a tarred road in all

this heat, back to Neuzen, which has a law court and timbered houses in the town center, while I drove on to Bundorp, a village where I've been working for months on a pig-headed garage proprietor. In the fields along the way there are a lot of oil pumps, and day and night they keep on working, the levers moving slowly up and down, automatically—a fantastic sight. The garage proprietor has a row of new, bright red tractors standing out in his yard for sale, and like many others in these parts he belongs to the shooting club. A number of painted carboard targets depicting stags or country scenes—trophies of his—are hanging on the walls of his office. That's the way they like it here.

This girl, though she is somewhat too young, will help me. I am forty now, and this is what I have been working toward, gradually accumulating strength, seeking my opportunities —for one tremendous outburst. And now I have met the girl. I have waited a long time, kept myself in check, intact, letting up now and again only to keep my hand in, because after all I am a man who is—and works to keep himself—fit. And now the hour of decision approaches. I know it, I feel it down to my fingertips as I sit here at the kitchen table, poised to spring. And I shall discharge it soundlessly, gloriously, visible to none but myself. The people in the development will not even notice. And that will be my triumph.

Yes, I can swim with her in the river, and take her into the bushes, where she will scream. I can give her clothes or the French racing bicycle. I can take her to my house, I can drive with her into the woods and fields, where no one can possibly hear her cries. I can choke her, fracture her wrists, tie her feet together, hang her up on a tree with fettered hands, beat her with a rod till she sobs and screams, strip off her clothes, slowly or quickly, tearing her dress to ribbons, drawing her blood and my blood. I can whip myself to a frenzy and take a stone or a knife to her, an ax, a hammer, shears, a bit of wire, or her own stockings if she should happen to be wearing any, which I doubt. I imagine exactly what I shall do. And the development will have no idea. I have a house of my own and I intend to keep it. That's something I have in common with the other dwellers in the development. It takes time and hard work to earn the right to sit safe and comfortable in your own house. There's nothing funny about that.

The fat woman has her boorish clod to fill her up, but I doubt whether she gives it much thought. To her it's like rain or dirty feet—something that goes with a clod you're married to and who worships eating. She's got her daughter, whose name for all I care is Brigitte, who is thin and who went swimming with me. But the mother pudding knows nothing about that. I'm one up there.

Get in, I said to her, it's Saturday, I'm calling it a day. Get in, can't you, what else have I got a car for? We can go for a drive, wherever you care to name, but we're not going swimming.

She was standing in the road a few miles outside Neuzen, a road that leads as far as I know to no lakes, rivers, or streams, but cuts clean across the heath and then on to Hamburg by way of Bergen and Lüneburg. I often use it, for my territory lies north of Neuzen as well. She got into the car.

Your feet are dirty, I said. That's because you always wear sandals. I could give you some stockings, but I suppose you're still too young for them. She seated herself beside me, and we drove off. She didn't want to tell me why she had been trudging in the heat along the tarred road again, keeping virtuously to the side facing oncoming traffic. Over her arm she had her usual little straw bag, which makes me want to look inside.

I just want to see things, she said, I don't yet know what I want to do. I found that very funny. I'm not in a hurry, she added. I won't kid myself that she'd been waiting on the road outside Neuzen just in order to meet me—waiting on a different road this time, so that I wouldn't catch on. Her mother is the most frightful person I know, though she doesn't really look any different from all the other women of her age in the development. I'm prejudiced, I suppose, because she's her mother.

They were all out on the road as they usually are on Saturdays, driving back and forth between the villages, jammed in tight with flushed faces and windows shut on account of the draft at the back. I often make faces at them when they come bowling past on the autobahn, solemn and superior, free of yearning and free of hunger. Gas tanks, bellies, and bladders filled up, all they want is to drive, to propel themselves along the autobahn or some other road like the one to Hamburg via Bergen and Lüneburg, sitting upright, cool or sweaty, with a stuffed tiger in the back window, a stuffed dwarf, a stuffed pelican, a stuffed deer, a stuffed stork, a cushion embroidered with car numbers. My rear window has a sticker label of the Grossglockner.

Before Bergen I turned off left beside a signpost with something carved or stamped on it—it looked like a camping sign. The paved road probably hadn't been there originally. I drove along it as far as the barracks. Above the entrance with its large wooden gate there is an arch on which you can read the initials of a Scottish regiment. In the courtyard behind stand the armored cars, the gun carriages, the trucks, all lined up precisely, and the soldiers who once liberated the camp now drill here, sweating, swinging their arms high, and marching a bit too fast and a bit too close together. And now we drive past in our cars while they, our victors and liberators, practice marching. It's sad really, and rather boring. She had never been here before, she said.

It's too far to walk in any case, I said. Have your parents never told you about it? It is after all a famous monument, I said, a beacon, a memorial ground, a sacrificial heath, or whatever you like to call it. But she was too young of course, I added charitably. She could not know, unless she had a television. Every Sunday afternoon throughout one summer they had broadcast a serial about that time, which I like anyone else of my age could remember of course, but not she. We drove along the bit of concrete that leads through the woods, the moorland woods. There the road turns off right to the shooting range. Practically all the heath is a restricted military area, shared by the British, the Americans, the Dutch, and ourselves for firing and tank practice. When do they fire the guns? she asked.

The former concentration camp is situated in the woods, as you would expect. It now has a large car park, a splendid car park, paved with concrete. At one end stands a long, low-built house, which interested me at first, but it turned out to be the visitors' washrooms. My little girl went in.

There were not many people there, and only about ten cars with Hamburg and Hanover license plates, besides one from Munich. Its occupants were leaning over a road map, and from their loud conversation I gathered they were on their way to Sweden. Of course, it was a Saturday. On Sunday there would certainly be more people there, but on weekdays most people are working. The camp is not on the autobahn either, which would make it easier to locate. The girl came back, plucking at her skirt.

I say nothing about golden drops, honey drops, water drops, drops of mucus, tongue tips, ear lobes, of firm narrow lips, short hairs, bits of gristle, stains, caresses, flowers in the mouth, knuckles, grass in the stomach, dirt in the pants, broken veins in the whites of the eyes. She was there again, swinging her handbag, and we walked straight across the magnificent car park to the entrance gate. This concentration camp is world-famous, I said.

The wide path is covered with fine gravel and sand, and on both sides there are grass borders. In front of these are low walls of uncut stone, and refuse containers. It all reminded me of the valley terminal of our cable railway back home. That also is generously laid out and bordered with uncut stone, and the path also leads in a gentle, easy curve through woodland scenery. Side by side we walked along, keeping in step and feeling perhaps rather solemn. That is how I felt, at any rate, for no one was taking photographs, and the few people there— two in front of us going the same way—kept quite silent. A couple was coming toward us. She had her head turned to the side, as if suppressing laughter. He—a tall fellow, taller than me and with a serious face—looked stern. As they came level with us, he leaned over toward me and in a deep, quiet voice, so even and quiet that he might have rehearsed it, he said, Your fly is open.

Then they had passed by, and I quickly pulled up the zipper. That often happens with me. The girl on my right looked away, but she is quick and bright, and I know now that she has a good head on her, for, though she is only fourteen, she at once began to ask a lot of questions, to help me over my embarrassment. When had the camp been built? Why had it been built? When would we begin to see things? She had seen nothing yet—it was just like a park. And I didn't know the answers.

Around the whole area of the camp runs a wire-mesh fence attached to concrete pillars. Along the top, where the pillars bend outwards, there is a strand of barbed wire. This fence is not original, of course. At any rate, that is what I told her.

But it's nice, she said, with all that heather everywhere and all that red sand on the paths. And over there the tennis courts, or rather playgrounds—or no, what are all those humps? We stood in front of a memorial—a sandstone tablet on which words were carved in Hebrew. Not that I could read them, but I heard some people near us saying that scrawls like that in a concentration camp must be in Hebrew. It certainly is impressive, the whole place—a huge assembly ground, an enormous clearing in the low-growing moorland wood, all of it on a slight slant. I was eager to know everything—after all, I had seen that television serial. I led the girl along the paths between the mounds, which are long and smooth and carefully rounded off at the sides—neat rectangular ramps covered with heather. Wherever I looked, to the left and right and farther along the path, there they stood, these hills, mounds, and ramps, and we hurried along between them, seized by an irresistible curiosity, a longing to be in on it at last, to catch a last dying spark. And then she saw some gravestones and crosses, strewn irregularly over a field, but a notice said they had nothing to do with the original scene. They were purely decorative, for show, and had been placed there at a later date. But they look right all the same.

That makes twenty thousand now, she said after the fourth mound. She continued adding them up and was disappointed when the slabs let into the brick facings at the foot of the mounds registered only two or three thousand corpses. All of the slabs bore the date March or April 45. Why? she asked.

We came to the cenotaph, built all in stone with an obelisk in front of a high wall, in which inscriptions were carved in several languages. What does it mean? she asked.

Maybe we'll see even more if we go to the back, I said, over to those birch trees. The heat, shimmering over the heather, beat down on us. A bit of a breeze would have been welcome. But the fever now had her in its grip too. She must get more corpses for her collection. Perhaps there were others behind the birches. We had already done the mounds. She ran on ahead.

The grounds are very quiet and well looked after. You can see that architects and gardeners have worked on them. You just can't leap about on the paths, so I did a sort of brisk walk, almost a trot. Everyone else was walking slowly and deliberately, arm in arm, holding their children by the hand. It made a pretty picture. The children, well behaved, gaily and lightly dressed, seemed to fit in this summer landscape, this perhaps slightly monotonous moorland park which was once a concentration camp, one of many and by no means a large one. In the television serial it had not even been mentioned.

Come on, she called out, here are some more graves. Here are some more bodies, she said as I stood beside her on a side path between the birches at the far end of the enclosure. We were once again on the same level as the cenotaph with the obelisk in front, and I saw now that the large clearing was in fact a hollow, a shallow dip, a plate with a raised rim supporting the false fence. So the grounds could be kept under observation from all sides. Clever, I found myself thinking. At least there's something written on these ones, she said. They're all foreigners here. What are they, she asked, Poles or French people or Russians? There was a star on all the others. Eagerly she searched around for more single graves. And then, among the birches, somewhere behind a hedge, she found another mound, containing seven thousand bodies. That was a record. It's much more than in both cemeteries in Neuzen put together, she said. True.

But it was something else that caught my attention. A track. Cutting straight through the clump of birches, straight through the false wire fence and far out into the heath in the direction of Bergen. It was still plain to see. There had been rails on it. It looked to me as if the birches had been planted later and the rails dismantled, as being out of keeping with a memorial ground. But there had been rails. I knew it because, where the ties had been, the grass was shorter. It had all grown over, but here and there the flints showed through—typical chippings of the sort the railway always uses for a roadbed. My heart began to thump. A branch line, I cried. Look, this is where the trains came in with their loaded cars, packed tight, the weak and sick below, the strong on top, where they had struggled up to the air holes. Look here, I shouted, shivering with excitement, you can see it all distinctly. The buffers stood here on this concrete block. This is where the trucks were unloaded. They had a good railway, right into the camp. I can't see anything, she said.

Then I discovered some broken masonry. Perhaps it had been a guardroom—certainly not a barrack hut, it was too small for that—and near it was a filled-in well. It could have been an officer's house. I seized the girl by the hand and plunged with her into the undergrowth, away from the neat path made for light shoes, through thorn bushes and brambles trailing along the ground. And there we found more masonry—hardly more than outlines hidden in the grass, long rectangles flanking the rails. Here at last was something I could grasp. I took bricks, scraps of metal, a rusty iron bar in my hands. It was all there from that time, lying in the bushes, invisible from the path. Here, I said, these were part of it. But it isn't much, not enough to make a proper picture of. This is where the camp guards lived, and down there were the incinerators. The wind blows right across the hollow from east to west. Though maybe they didn't burn them, but shot them, or used spades or knives or axes. I felt helpless, confused, I could have wept. Why can't they write it up on a notice board, for Christ's sake? I couldn't really *see* it. The heat lay thick in the bushes. Both of us were sweating. We could no longer hear whether there were people on the path. I was almost sick with excitement. She was somewhere behind me, making dents in the ground maybe with her heels, picking flowers or counting the bees. But for me she was coming from the river, clean and slim, quick and agile. She was swinging a birch, a cane, a stick, some sort of stake, a whip, a cudgel, a steel rod, a wooden mallet. This is where the guards had lived, and over there the convoys had come in. Here they had sorted them, the young and pretty ones, the heavy and fleshy women—they hadn't been fat, lean rather—had perhaps put them aside for a few days, I thought, and in spite of the heat in the bushes I was shivering. Alone, in twos or threes or in groups even, they had done all the things you could think of, sharing the women out, singly or maybe not—what did it matter when the supply was so large, inexhaustible? At any time they could be sent off down to the hollow, to the pits or the stakes. God, I could scarcely breathe. I dared not look around for the girl, who was standing behind me, I knew, for now I could see it all—everything imaginable. I hadn't been a guard, hadn't ever worked there —of course I hadn't—but I can see her there among them, I can see myself picking her out, binding her, cutting myself a switch, suspending her by the hands from the bedpost. Food and drink I'd have given her, locked up there in the room, wine and bread, but her clothes she'd have had to keep on—and I'd have put a dog over her, they were trained to do it too—but then I'd have packed her off, down to the rest of them in the hollow, whoever was there at the time, for I couldn't have stood it for long—not all this richness and fulfillment which a man can have for nothing, gloriously free. Come, let's go, I said.

In the lovely car park we found a mobile shop which someone had trailed behind a car. I bought some raspberry drops for myself and a chocolate-coated ice for her. She pressed it cautiously with her teeth till the glazing cracked. I asked the man at the mobile shop how long the memorial park had been there, but he had come to Bergen only two years earlier and didn't know. He was usually out here on fine weekends, he told us, for a lot of buses came with schoolchildren and tourists. We got in my car and drove off, not back toward Bergen but on through the woods along the smooth concrete road, from which tracks to both sides cut across the heath to the practice areas for shooting and tank driving. There were signposts with various abbreviations on them and warnings that the woods were a restricted area. It was a pleasant drive, through villages of old houses with thatched roofs and huge entrance doors under the gables. In one village there was a clump of broad oak trees on the green. A leafy cathedral, I said, let's get out and take a look at the trees. But she wanted to see the fishponds near Meschede, which meant a detour, and then the ponds were empty. It was a waste of time.

Looking down from my upstairs room on the street in which her house stands, on the very edge of the development, I have to laugh when I think how I drove straight to it. She was sitting beside me, no longer stirring. She got out. I reversed and turned the car around, then drove back to my own house. I got out and locked it, went through the gate, through the garden, into the house through the front door, and locked the door behind me.

It really is ridiculous. None of them can possibly conceive what is going on in my imagination. What I hear, what I feel in my mouth, what my fingers are itching to do—they know nothing. I am the only person in the whole development—at least, I hope I am—who can keep so much stored up inside, who has the power, should he wish—I shout it aloud—to destroy himself. God, what utter ecstasy, what indescribable glory, to do all you have it in you to do, before they strike you dead! Thank you very much for the drive, she said.

Here are the houses, all identical—front gardens, flower beds, wire fences, rabbit hutches, string beans, chives, onions, radishes, cabbage patches, scooters, bicycles, and sometimes a car in a shed out back. There are grandmothers, a few grandfathers, mothers, fathers, some with children, some without. Her name is Brigitte.

It makes me wild with rage, it sets my teeth on edge to think of them gossiping together, breathing to each other what sort of person I am, making plans, uttering warnings, drinking beer, playing cards and cursing as they bang down the jack of clubs or the ace of diamonds on the table, messing up the crossword puzzle and writing in the wrong words because they are so busy thinking about me. We might go for another drive sometime, I said. We shall see.

But I'm not going to give her that racing bicycle. I imagine her riding it. I see her wide skirt flapping, her sinewy legs pressing on the pedals, knees revolving, skinny arms stretched to the handlebars. Beneath her skirt the white panties sit a bit loose on the thighs and flutter. On the hard saddle she jigs from side to side, in these panties wrongly called bloomers, which show the darns and are no longer quite white. Would you like me to give you a bicycle? I said.

The café lies across the street from the milk bar to which the youngsters go. You see them standing till shortly before eight o'clock in front of the door, wondering whether or not to go to the movie, for the movie house is just around the corner beside the vocational high school. I sometimes go to the café and sit at a little table in the alcove near the window overlooking the road. Neuzen's main street leads to "our theater," as everyone here calls it. They are all proud of the palace with the moat and the lawns around it—the yellow palace which has a theater but no prince. They are proud, too, of the courthouse and its great auditorium, which has a gallery and a painted ceiling carved by hand. It is unique.

In the café I can get cakes with polka dots on top, which I like to eat with a cup of cocoa and a schnapps. That's why I sometimes go there. He was standing on the pavement before the milk bar. There was nothing particularly striking about him. I just happened to see him standing there. The movie had already begun, or perhaps he had just come from there. He had black hair and in his hand he carried a little radio, a transistor, a trashy sort of thing in a leather case with holes for the sound. From my table I couldn't of course hear whether he had it turned on or not. It didn't look as if he were listening to the news, though maybe he was—to the "freedom" station over in the East Zone. The reception is quite good here, and it broadcasts all the latest song hits interspersed with short news items, usually with the accent on crime, and delivered in a rapid, breathless way which makes you listen, though it's probably all lies anyway.

A young man, or rather a boy, a scatter-brained kid of not more than nineteen, standing there in front of the milk bar, shifting from one leg to the other. Well, I was young once too, and ready for anything—in fact, I still am, because I'm lean and go swimming in every water hole I see. I know his sort—they can do it both ways. There's a woman who keeps a store for used furniture from army stocks and officers' houses, and she was telling me about a lawyer with a hunting lodge near Hünsdorf who was caught with a kid like that by the area gamekeeper, who had come to see him. They were quarreling, and the lawyer's boy friend, who wasn't by any stretch of imagination a hairdresser or a tailor's assistant, but a trainee at the town hall, was demanding more money. He stood there in a raincoat and the lawyer in pajamas, while the gamekeeper watched and wondered. He described it all in detail to this woman at the furniture store, who has a policy with me. Strike me dead, she said, if it isn't true.

She went straight up to him, walking with little short steps—not like on the tarred road—handbag swinging on her arm. She veered toward him a bit too quickly and stopped. I sat at my table and stabbed my fork into the pastry, breaking it into little pieces. I saw everything that went on between him and the girl who for all I care is named Brigitte. There they stood in front of the milk bar and smiled at each other, and he made a sign with his head, and she nodded, and together they went into the teen-ager milk bar called the Cabin.

What should I do? I could go across to the milk bar and sit

down at a table and wait for her to greet me. Or I could greet her first, or simply sit down at her table. And then what? I might just as well stay where I was in the café. I ordered another slice of cake.

Does the mother hen know about it? I could tell her, I could make an alliance with her, work out a plot with her, ingratiate myself, I could bring her seedlings for the garden, ask her about the neighbors, question her so as to find out what is happening in the development. She would thaw out, chatter and complain, and pearls of sweat would drip down the chasm of her whopping breasts. That would be fun—with daughter darling there in the kitchen as well, and I could pinch her surreptitiously, because I should be sitting on the sofa too.

But the pain, which I do not yet feel sharply enough, the pain would make me proud and exalted perhaps, as I follow her about, wait for her in the car at the gate, go into the milk bar and sit down at her table, talk to her and offer her gifts like the bicycle, go swimming with her, creep through the bushes with my camera and afterwards give her the pictures, developed far away in Brunswick—as, sitting beside me, she pushes away my hand and with a scornful smile sniffs through her nose, arches her back, stretching tight her blouse, her pullover, her dress, her raincoat. All this she can do, for it's all the same to her what she'll do later, she can do what she has to do with me or with others, willing and eager, until I have had enough. Can we meet again tomorrow? I would say.

I sit in my kitchen in which I also sleep, though I have a whole house to myself. I live in the development because the house is mine and I can afford no other. I could turn on television—later on I certainly shall. I could position myself in one of the rooms upstairs with a telescope, and wait to see if she comes out and walks down the street past my house to the place where somebody is waiting—that or another boy or some kid from the vocational high school who won't ever become an engineer but just a salesman for tractors and sowing machines. Stop there, I would say, and point the gun.

But I have no gun, and am thankful for it. Great pain is dangerous—it obscures my purpose and demands attention for itself. And that is not what I want. I shall go swimming and imagine myself in Bergen, imagine it as I swim, lying on my back, paddling and pushing my way around the sandbanks to the whirlpool and back, imagine it deep in the bushes with the buzzing heat and the decapitating rod, where there was once a concentration camp which is now a memorial park, where—I can imagine it better back home in the kitchen—where I beat her bloody, drive matchsticks under her toenails, plane her and peel her, gradually getting her ripe for my great and glorious eruption, the noise of which will bring them all running to my house, their hands still clutching cards, knitting needles, breadknives, which they will drop, because they cannot believe what I have done. Not they.

Tomorrow I shall drive out to Klüversen, another place where oil has been struck. The towers are already in position in the middle of the potatoes, the rye and oatfields, with solid hip-high fences and notices bearing the name of the firm. Around them the farmers reap and plow and stack and weed and draw a fraction of a penny for every gallon that's pumped or sold on an average reckoning. It all means more houses—dream houses in a housing development, houses in the style of the local farms or the gasoline stations, houses like those in my prospectuses, reasonable in price and payable in many installments. That is where I shall go.

I am getting my profit from the country too, from this monotonous, flat countryside of heath and birch and oak and fields between villages and towns with names like Meschede, Neuzen, Womsrode, Niensen, Macholz, Tinglam, Umsdorf, Hameden and Lüneburg, Soltau and Bostel. I have my house in the development.